Annie Dreaming

Carley Eason Evans

ANNIE DREAMING

1 - DEEP CUT

The day is gray, overcast. Not a sliver of blue anywhere. Annie presses her cheek to the windowpane and watches her brothers in the backyard. Rick pitches to Charlie, who is the catcher. *Charlie's always catcher. Always.* Annabelle, as her mother calls her, feels the cold against her cheek as she counts the number of times Charlie catches the baseball. She loses count after Charlie catches the twenty-fifth pitch. Finally, Rick stops, turns towards the house. He looks tired. Even through the glass, Annie can hear his booming voice. He says, "That's enough Charlie. Go do your homework." Annie barely hears Charlie's protest, but she knows her brother wants to keep catching pitches. But, Charlie relents. He gets up out of his crouch and limps a little at first, then bends his knees up to his chest a few times. Afterwards, he jogs to the back door, opens it.

"Hey there Annie-belle," he says to her. She gazes into her brother's eyes. She smiles, says, "Hey there, Charlie." Just as Rick so often ruffles Charlie's curly hair, Charlie ruffles his little sister's hair, then goes off somewhere in the house. Annie looks back to the yard. Rick stands near the fence, his hands over his face; his head leaning slightly against one of the fence boards. Annie doesn't understand. Rick stands there, very still except for the shaking. Rain begins to splatter the glass; soon Annie can't see through the streaks. Not long though, the back door opens and a wet Rick enters the back foyer where he stamps his feet. He glances at Annie. "Hi Annabelle."

Then he quickly moves to the half bathroom off the kitchen. He shuts the door; Annie hears it lock.

Annie waits by the window for Rick to exit the bathroom. She wants to read Rick's eyes to see if he's okay. She doesn't fully understand; but nobody stands out in the rain. She knows that much.

The baseball is big as the moon when it strikes her forehead. She feels it, then knows she's falling. The ground, when she hits it, is soft with green grass but also hard with rocks and dirt. She doesn't cry. She feels her breath go shallow. Charlie is there; he's crying. She hears him call her name over and over. She hears her own voice, richer than she's ever known, say: *Hush Charlie; it's okay. I'm okay.*

The bathroom door unlocks. Rick comes out, but he won't look at Annie. He walks by her into the kitchen. Annie follows him with her eyes, but she can't see her brother's face. She can't tell if he's okay. She gets up, and goes after him.

In the kitchen, their mother cooks dinner. She taps the wooden spoon against the side of the pot, puts it down, turns and carefully picks up Annabelle. "Hey baby! Dinner's almost ready. You hungry?"

"Yes ma'am," says Annie.

"Okay, sweetie." Judith puts her daughter down. "Set the table. I put the dishes out for you." And her mother points to the big round wooden table where the dishes are stacked.

"Yes ma'am."

Annie sets the table. She folds the napkins and places the silverware. She puts a glass on the right side of Charlie's plate; the glass hits the side of the porcelain dish and cracks, shattering in her hand. The blood surprises her.

Her mother is right there, immediately wrapping a wet towel around her hand. Rick picks up Annabelle.

"How bad is it?" he asks his mother.

Their mother lifts the towel, soaked in blood. She looks at her son, "Looks pretty deep."

"I'll get the keys to the truck, Mom."

"Oh good. Let's go."

Rick reaches over, turns off the stove, keeping Annabelle from the heat rising from the eye. He grabs the Chevy truck keys from the hook on the wall near the back door.

Annie's mother yells, "Charlie. Charles! We're taking Annabelle to the emergency room. Stay here. I need you to call your father. Charles? Charlie!"

Charlie appears in the kitchen doorway. "What happened?"

Rick says, "Annabelle cut open her hand."

His mother says, "You stay here. Call your father. Tell him that I can't pick him up. Tell him we went to the hospital. I'll try to call you when we know something."

With that, Rick carries Annie to the truck. Their mother follows behind, gets in the driver's side while Rick scoots into the passenger side with Annie in his lap. Richard hands his mother the keys. Judith starts the Chevy, cautiously backs out of the driveway.

Charlie stands in the rain for a few moments before going back into the house.

When his father comes home, he finds Charlie sitting at the kitchen table doing his math homework. Charlie's put a cover on the food still waiting on the stove, having decided not to eat alone. Jim glares at his son. "What? Did y'all eat without me?"

Charlie glances up. His father is wet. *The man never seems to have an umbrella when he needs one.* "No sir," says Charlie. "Annie cut her hand. Mom and Rick took the Chevy to - Oh gosh, I forgot to call you!"

"You certainly did," says Jim. "I had to walk to the bus stop, wait in the rain for the damn thing; then walk home from King - two blocks over!" And Jim raises his hand momentarily as if to strike his son, then drops it. Charlie's eyes widen. Jim says, "Never mind."

Jim goes into the bathroom just as Charlie mumbles an apology. Charlie rises, walks to the stove, stirs the contents of the pot, flips the gas switch over so that the eye lights. Looks like some sort of chicken and vegetable stew to him. His mother is not a gourmet cook; she only manages to put nutritious food on the table. He puts the lid back on the pot.

Annie-belle sits up, feels the welt forming in the middle of her forehead. Charlie still cries. *Hush there now Charlie. I'm okay. Look, I'm here.*

At the hospital, once the blood flow is under control, Annabelle needs four stitches in her palm. She gets a lollipop from the nurse at the emergency room. The woman smiles at her. "You're very brave, little lady."

"Yes ma'am," says Annie.

Her mother pays, and then drives them home.

Jim waits in the living room. He's reading the paper when the front door opens. Rick carries Annabelle into the foyer and upstairs while Judith joins her husband on the couch. She leans in close, gives Jim a kiss on the cheek. He puts the paper down, turns to her and gives her a full kiss on the lips.

"You all right?"

"I'm exhausted," she admits.

"Charles forgot to call me."

"Oh no," says Judith. "How'd you get home?"

"The damn bus."

"I'm sorry, Jim."

"Not your fault." And with that, he turns back to his newspaper.

2 - NEWS READ

The Vietnam War is the central story on the nightly news, and Rick fears that one day he is going to be called up to serve in the jungles of Southeast Asia. He leans his head against the fence, realizes how much he doesn't want to fight. *Maybe the war will end before I am called up. Maybe I can be a conscientious objector.* He laughs at himself. He doesn't even believe in God. And he's not a pacifist. Instead, he's afraid to die. He notices he's shaking. It starts to rain. He stands there, getting soaked. Eventually, he goes inside the house, stamps his feet in the foyer, tries to avoid Annabelle who is waiting for him. He still says "hi" to her, but he's curt. He goes into the bathroom, dries his hair with one of his mother's hand towels. He looks at himself; he's handsome. He knows it. His mother calls. Dinner is ready.

Annabelle's setting the table. He hears the glass shatter. The blood surprises him as it surprises his sister. Their mother is fast; a wet towel around Annabelle's hand in moments. Yet, blood covers the plate and the white tablecloth.

A helicopter blade slices the air. Rick hears it screech as the metal bends; smoke pours into the cargo bay as the engine explodes. *We're going down. This is it. This is what I've been afraid of for years.*

Rick swoops in, picks up Annabelle and yells to his mother that he has the keys to the truck. His mother shouts to Charlie, who is somewhere in the house. She tells him to call their dad who obviously needs to find another way home. *I won't be able to pick up Jim.*

Judith drives too slowly to the hospital, but traffic is light so they get there quickly anyway; and this is good. The doctor examines Annabelle's hand - the cut is deep; the blood flow continuous. Annabelle cries when the doctor stitches her hand. The nurse gives her a cherry lollipop. Cherry is her favorite flavor. She falls asleep in Rick's arms. He can't drive the truck, so Judith does. She rarely drives Jim's Chevy except to drop off and pick up her husband at his insurance office on days she might need the truck. The Chevy means so much to the man; she's terrified she might wreck. Rick shakes his head. "Mom," he says, "you're fine. You're a good driver. Don't worry."

So Judith scoots in behind the wheel of the Chevy while Rick climbs into the passenger side with Annabelle asleep against his shoulder, her legs straddling his lap. She's softly snoring, exhausted from blood loss and mild shock.

Judith drives too slowly again. Her son tells her so. She laughs nervously when she finally manages to park the truck in the driveway of the house. When she opens the front door, she sees Jim on the couch reading his newspaper. She joins him, leans in close, kisses him on the cheek. He kisses her lips, his tongue briefly finding hers. She stirs.

Jim interrupts their kiss, complains, "Charles forgot to call me."

Judith asks how he got home, and Jim angrily tells her about the bus ride. Judith thinks, *he hates that bus.* She decides not to let on that she drives the Chevy too slowly again both going to and coming back from the hospital. Her husband generously tells her it's not her fault that he has to ride the city bus home from work.

Rick comes into the living room. "Excuse me, you two. I've put Annabelle to bed, but she's restless. You ought to check on her, Mom."

Judith says, "Of course." She rises, leaves the two.

Rick sits next to his father, who picks up his paper and starts to read again. Rick waits a moment, then says, "Dad, I'm really scared."

Jim reads to the end of the paragraph, then turns to look at his oldest son, who is nevertheless still very young to be concerned about going to a war on the other side of the world. Jim asks, "Why?"

"I keep having this same dream - over and over - " Rick swallows hard. He glances into his father's eyes. The man looks back. "I see this helicopter. Well, not exactly. I'm in this helicopter. I may even be the pilot. I'm not sure. The engine explodes, but first I hear this awful screeching noise, like metal rubbing against metal. And then smoke everywhere. And then we're falling. And I'm dead."

Jim waits about fifteen seconds before speaking. To Rick, those seconds seem to fill the room with a heaviness he can't understand much less shake. His father finally responds, "Well, Rick. That's quite a dream."

Is that all you've got to say? That's it? That's the whole of your fatherly wisdom?

His father raises the newspaper and re-reads the last sentence of the last paragraph of the article he started earlier. The article is about the devastating effects of Napalm with an oh-so brief mention of Agent Orange.

3 - FACE DOWN

Charlie waits upstairs in bed for the house to go dark, for his parents to fall asleep, for Rick to stop his hunt and peck typing in their father's downstairs office. Then, he rises and goes to Annie's room. The door is cracked part-way open. He peers inside. In the tiny glow from the nightlight, Charlie can see his sister is sound asleep. He watches her chest rise and fall. He sighs. *She's okay. She's not going to leave me.* Charlie goes back to bed, sleeps easily for the rest of the night.

In the morning, Annie is up early. She crawls out of bed, goes down into the kitchen where her mother is making pancakes. Her hand is stiff, and hurts.

"Mommy," says Annie. "It hurts." And she holds up her bandaged hand.

Judith says, "I can't stop right this second, honey. I'm in the middle of flipping this pancake. When I get this one done, I'll turn off the heat and see if I can make it better. Okay?"

"Okay, Mommy."

Annie sits at the kitchen table and pulls at the bandage. Her mother flips the pancake, takes it off the skillet, puts it on a plate and turns off the heat. Then, she sits next to Annabelle. "Don't do that, sweetie. Let me." Annie holds out her hand; her mother gets up, gathers the first aid supplies the hospital provides. When she unwraps the bandage; the layer next to the wound has stuck to the stitches. When Judith pulls it away, Annabelle starts to cry.

"Mommy! Mommy! Don't!" screams Annabelle.

Charlie wakes with a start. He hears Annie from the kitchen. She's crying. He rubs his eyes, swings his legs over the edge of the bed, and sits there a moment. He hears Annie scream. He rises, goes downstairs quickly. When he enters the kitchen, his mother and sister are at the table. His mother tries to get Annabelle to calm down. Charlie comes close, sits on the other side of Annie, and hugs her. Annie stops crying. She leans on her brother's shoulder, and her voice cracks as she says, "Oh, Charlie. It hurts."

"I know it does, Annie-belle. But Mom is going take care of you, okay?"

Annie looks into Charlie's eyes. She sighs deeply. "Okay, Charlie. Okay." Then she holds out her hand for her mother, who pulls the rest of the bandage from Annabelle's palm. A little blood sprouts at the edge of the cut. Annie squeezes her eyes shut, and turns her head toward her brother. Judith finishes up, adding a dab of antibiotic cream and re-bandaging the wound.

"All done," says Judith.

Charlie says, "See Annie; that wasn't so bad."

"No, it hurt." And Annie buries her face in Charlie's shoulder. He pats her head, strokes her long hair. He glances at his mother. Judith has gone back to making pancakes, turning the eye back on, now pouring batter onto the hot griddle. She says to Charlie, her back to him and to Annie: "How many do you want, Charles?"

Charles. I can't refuse the pancakes. He says, "I'll take four small ones, Mom or two big ones."

Judith responds, "Four it is."

Her mother, Susan, never makes pancakes - not once. Judith watches the bubbles form and collapse; she flips the last pancake, then puts it on the stack. She turns to put the platter on the table. Annie is sound asleep against Charlie's chest. Charlie's chin rests atop Annie's head. Judith is surprised to see that both her children are asleep.

4 - BASIC TRAINING

Charlie Logan plays for his high school baseball team, the Springboro Panthers. He's one of Coach Coffey's best catchers. He's not a very good batter, but he holds his own. In his crouch behind home plate, however, he's stellar. He catches virtually any pitch, any batter-deflected ball, any fly thrown in from the outfield. Charlie believes he's a good catcher because of his big brother, Rick. Rick spends every afternoon after school and most Saturday mornings practicing with him in the backyard or on the public ball field in the township park. When Rick leaves for basic training, Charlie slips into boredom, especially on Saturdays. *Hard to catch a ball no one pitches.*

Rick loves Charlie; that's why he pitches baseballs every afternoon and nearly every Saturday morning all through Charlie's elementary, middle and high school years. But it is their father Jim who first tosses a ball to Charlie, who is 4 and holding a bat much too large and heavy for him. Jim pitches a clean fast ball at his son, who swings hard and misses. Jim yells, "Keep your eyes on the ball, Charles!"

"Yes, Daddy."

"Here's another one. Now watch it, son."

The ball sails by Charlie in a flash of white. Charlie stands there, smiles at his dad, who yells at him again. "What's wrong with you? Keep your eye on the ball!"

Charlie almost sings, "Yes, Daddy."

The baseball flies by his swing again as he mistimes it. Suddenly, his father stands over him, his arm raised back for the strike which makes contact with Charlie's right ear. The hand is flat so it lands as a slap not a punch. Nevertheless the blow knocks Charlie sideways. He falls onto the ground and hits his head. Just like in afternoon cartoons, he sees little stars dance around his forehead. He stifles his tears, refusing to allow them access to his cheeks. *No, no, no - you can't come out to play. No, no, no - not today!* He gets up, swings the bat back and stands ready for the next pitch. Jim looks at his son, walks back a distance, turns, and lets fly another fast pitch. Charlie swings, missing the baseball once more.

Jim says in disgust, "You can't do it, Charles. Might as well accept it!" And his father throws the ball into the dirt at his feet, goes into the house. Charlie stands, waits a few moments before he drops the bat and follows his father.

The very next weekend, Jim pulls his son out of bed early on Saturday; barks at him: "Get up; get dressed. You're gonna learn to hit today."

Charlie rubs his face; the sleep comes out of the corners of his eyes. "Yes, Daddy." Jim tosses a tee-shirt and shorts that don't match onto Charlie's bed. "Here," he says, "put these on. Mush. Mush. Let's go."

Charlie gets out of his bed, looks up at his father, says, "Yes, Daddy."

Jim crosses his arms, watches his son hurriedly dress. He barks again, "Come on, let's go."

Charlie looks at his father again. "Yes, Daddy."

"Come down to the kitchen when you get done."

"Okay, Daddy."

Jim leaves Charlie, who goes to the bathroom in the hall. His bladder is full; he holds the urine as long as possible while his father stands over him urging him to get dressed as fast as possible. Charlie lifts the toilet lid and pees; some urine gets on the seat. *Mommy won't like that.* He pulls paper off the toilet roll and wipes the seat. He flushes the toilet, stands on the wooden step at the sink so he can reach the faucet handles. He turns on the water, washes his hands. When he gets done, he remembers to brush his teeth and put the comb through his tight curly hair.

He runs downstairs to find Jim at the kitchen table with a cup of hot coffee. His father blows on the surface of it, then sips. "You ready, champ?"

Champ? Charlie doesn't know this word. "Yes, Daddy." He's hungry but he doesn't tell his father. He looks at the half-eaten piece of toast on his father's plate. He reaches out to take it, stops, asks his father if it's okay. "Well sure, Charlie. Go ahead. Want another one, one of your own?"

"Yes, Daddy."

"Okay," says Jim. He stands, unwraps the loaf of bread, pulls out a piece and places it in the toaster. He pushes the black lever down and sits back at the table. He picks up his newspaper, begins to read. Charlie hesitates, then sits next to his father at the table. He waits for the toaster to ding as the toast pops up. When it does, Jim doesn't react. Charlie waits. Suddenly, Jim folds his paper, puts it on the table, turns to his son, says, "Okay, let's do this." Charlie glances at the toast that's growing colder. His stomach growls. He nods at his father, who says, "Last one to the truck is a rotten egg."

Charlie grins. He chases after his father who bolts toward the side door. Charlie is not able to keep up with his father much less beat him to the truck. Jim waits on the passenger side; when Charlie arrives he picks him up and swings him into the truck, buckles the seatbelt and laughs, "Okay champ; we're off!" The baseball bat and ball and something Charlie's not seen in the truck before are on the floorboard.

He points, "What's that, Daddy?"

Jim leans over, looks down. "Oh, that's a glove, Charles."

"A glove?"

"A mitt, Charles. A baseball player's mitt."

"A mitt?"

"Yes, Charles - for catching the baseball."

Catching the baseball?

5 - PLAYING CATCH

Charlie doesn't learn to hit a baseball when he is 4 years old, but he does learn he loves the smell and the feel of the mitt in his nose and on his hand. The glove Jim owns doesn't fit Charlie's little hand, but Charlie likes to wear it anyway. His kindergarten teacher tells Judith to make Charlie leave the glove at home. She says, "He can't finger paint with a baseball glove on his hand." Judith shakes her head, but says she'll keep the glove at home. Charlie is reluctant to leave it, but stops coming to school with the golden leather mitt.

Jim offers to pitch to his son only if Charles is willing to hold a bat. So Charlie asks Rick, who resists at first. *Who wants to spend their afternoons and Saturdays with their little brother anyway?*

"Please Rick," asks Charlie several times.

"Okay, Charlie."

Even a young Rick recognizes Charlie is a natural. While Charlie has difficulty keeping his eyes on the ball coming at the bat, a long extension of himself; he has no trouble watching the ball come to his glove hand. The glove and Charlie's hand are one and the same, it seems to Rick. *It's like the catcher's mitt is an extension of Charlie's arm.*

On the first day Rick pitches to his little brother, the baseball finds its own way to the glove or so it seems to both brothers.

Whatever kind of pitch Rick throws, Charlie's glove is there to intercept the baseball. Charlie's not yet out of kindergarten, so he doesn't fully comprehend what looks like a miracle to Rick who is a few years older.

"That's amazing!" screams Rick in a high-pitched voice.

"Do it again!" cries Charlie.

Again and again, Rick pitches and Charlie catches the baseball. Each time the ball smacks the sweet spot of the mitt, Charlie thrills to the feel and the sound. *So good. So good.*

Turtle Creek Township doesn't have a Little League team, so Charlie continues to catch pitches from Rick. He and his brother try to get their father to join them, but Jim refuses. He manages to distract Rick, too. He gets Rick interested in working on the Chevy truck. Sometimes Rick pitches to Charlie only half an hour before going to the garage to tinker under the hood of Jim's truck. The Chevy is just a year old when Rick starts to fool around with the cables. The first week, he disconnects the distributor cap accidentally, but figures out how to reconnect it in no time. He's a whiz at auto mechanics the same way Charlie is at catching baseballs. Jim is thrilled. Rick is mesmerized.

Rick changes the oil, stretched out beneath the truck engine. He drains out the old, then funnels in the new. He changes the filter, too. He's covered in oil when he comes to dinner. Judith exhales sharply when she sees his black smudged face.

"Richard Logan!" she cries. "Wash up!"

"Yes ma'am."

When he washes his hands, his mother's white soap turns grey with muck; the oil adheres to the bar. The grey sludge in the sink worries Rick. He glances at the hand towel; it's yellow. If he puts his hands to it, he'll ruin it. He stands, holding his arms up so that the dirty grey soap begins to run down to his wrists and onto his forearms. *What am I going to do?*

He yells through the wooden bathroom door. "Hey Mom! Mom!"

"What is it, son?" His father's voice comes from the back foyer.

"I need a shop towel, Dad."

His father rattles the door handle. Rick stares at it. "Open the goddamn door, Richard."

"I can't, Dad."

The voice on the other side is shrill. "Open the door, Richard. Now!" And a thud toward the bottom of the door indicates to Rick his father has struck it with his booted foot.

"My hands, Dad. I need a shop towel. Shove it under the door."

Rick hears his father mutter, walk away. A few moments later, Judith's voice comes through the door. "What's wrong, Rick?"

Rick explains. His mother tells him she'll be right back with the shop towel. Rick puts his hands in the sink, waits. A few minutes later, the shop towel appears at his feet, its edge peeking under the door.

6 - BABY TIME

Quite by accident, Rick and Charlie discover their mother is going to have another child. Both come in one afternoon after a serious game of catch to find Judith on the telephone in the kitchen. She asks the anonymous person on the other end of the line, "When am I due?"

Rick looks at Charlie, winks. Charlie says, "What?" He doesn't understand the implication of his mother's words. On the other hand, Rick knows. He tells his little brother. Charlie's eyes widen and he smiles. The two boys keep their secret knowledge between them.

Late in Judith's pregnancy, the women of Turtle Creek Methodist church arrange a baby shower in the basement of the sunday school building. The many gifts are appreciated by both Jim and Judith. However, as usual, only the women of the church take notice of the birth of the Logan's third child. The men don't know Jim well. Those who notice him long enough think he's standoffish. Others see him as a sour man; a few think Jim is boring and perhaps a little stupid. On the other hand, everyone in the church loves the warm, friendly Judith Logan.

A few months later, a baby girl is born. Jim and Judith name her Annabelle Louise Logan. When she is introduced to Charlie, he says, "She's pretty." From the day he first sees Annie, Charlie thinks his sister's eyes are wide and fully open to him; and he enjoys playing with her hair, curly like his own.

One afternoon, their mother places baby Annabelle on a pink blanket on the couch, and asks Charlie to keep an eye on her. "Don't let her roll off, Charlie."

"I won't."

"Good boy," says Judith as she leaves the living room for a quick stop in the bathroom. She listens intently as she sits on the toilet. No alarming sound comes to her ears. She relaxes. She flushes the toilet, washes her hands, comes back to find Charlie stretched out beside his little sister. He looks up at Judith, and says, "She's sleeping Mommy. Look."

Sure enough, Annabelle is fast asleep.

"You're a good babysitter, Charlie. Thank you." Judith thinks better of her statement, says, "You're a great big brother, Charles."

Charlie's really proud. He likes helping his mother. Annabelle's soft face next to his own makes him love her more than he thought possible. After all, sometimes Annabelle screams, inconsolable and angry. Sometimes she stinks, and he doesn't want to be around her when Judith changes her diaper. But here stretched out beside her softness, Charlie loves his baby sister so much.

7 - BLACK CAR

Rick is in Vietnam only a month when he's involved in the Cedar Falls Operation. He gets the call, climbs into his jumpsuit, settles his helmet, flicks on the headset microphone and receiver, runs to his Huey helicopter. As he climbs aboard to take his seat as pilot, a cold sweat forms on his face, neck and shoulders. His stomach cramps, and he's nauseous. The last time he climbs into the pilot's seat on this very helicopter, he has the same feeling. As a matter of fact, every time he climbs into this helicopter he has this weight on his stomach. *This is it. This time. I'm going to die.*

The flight is long; Rick settles in. The nausea subsides. He begins to relax. Then, they are taking fire from a stand of trees. *Jungle trees; look like palms.* Rick hears the screech of the helicopter blades, sees one curling down to scrape against the front of the bird. Then a mighty shudder and the craft is falling. *Oh my; this really is it.*

When Judith sees the black car from the kitchen window, she faints. Jim is at work in his insurance office, meeting a new client - a young man in need of health insurance for his growing family. Charles and Annabelle are in school, so Judith is alone. The two military men knock at the front door, then come around to the side door off the garage. They bang on the glass panes set in the top of the door. "Anyone home?" One of the men sees Judith sprawled on the floor. He takes his cap from his head, secures it around his fist which he punches through the lowest pane. He reaches in to unlock the door.

Both men come into the kitchen. One finds a hand towel, wets it, and gently places it across the woman's forehead.

"Ma'am? Are you okay, ma'am?"

Judith stirs. She looks at the two men in dress uniform and begins to cry softly. Between sobs, she manages to ask even as she dreads the inevitable answer. "Yes ma'am," says the first officer as he helps Judith to a chair at the wooden table. "We regret to inform you that your son, Richard Lewis Logan is listed as 'missing in action.' His helicopter went down during the Cedar Falls Operation yesterday."

Judith asks the older of the two men to call the school and let Charles know. She forgets about telling Jim. All she can think of is Charlie in the backyard catching baseballs. *Poor Charles.* Then Judith blankly stares at the surface of the table. The two men look at each other. "Ma'am?"

Judith looks up at the young soldier, "Yes?"

"Oh, okay." He stumbles momentarily. "I wasn't sure you were with us."

"Did you call the school?"

The other soldier answers, "Yes ma'am. I just hung up." He looks at her closely. "Your son is on the field, but I let the coach know. I'm sure he'll tell him to come on home."

Judith nods her thanks. The two men hesitate, glance at each other; then excuse themselves and drive away in the black car. Judith looks up at the clock face. She stares at the second hand as it circles.

8 - LESSER HOUSEHOLD

Judith's father, Michael Lesser grows up outside Beckley, West Virginia. His father, George Lesser is a coal miner and dies of Black Lung at the young age of 49. Michael refuses work in the mines, runs from home at the age of 14.

At a local cafe in Beckley, Michael meets Judith's mother, Susan Holmes who waits on him one early Sunday morning. Her smile infectious, Michael touches her hand as she sets his plate of eggs, bacon, and grits on the counter in front of him. He winks when she glances at his face. Susan's entire countenance goes red with the blush of her embarrassment. Michael manages to ask her out on a date, and she surprises him with a soft and quiet, "Yes." They go to a Big Band dance at the local hall. Michael, although handsome and charming, is barely able to dance. Susan helps him out as much as she can, but he steps on her toes several times anyway.

For Susan, falling in love with Michael is easy. While he courts her, Michael is sweet and generous. He gives her fresh daises which he picks from roadsides. When he has extra cash, he likes to buy the little trinkets Susan sees in shop windows on their Saturday afternoon strolls through downtown Beckley. Susan hesitates to accept his gifts, but Michael insists.

On the other hand, getting married is difficult as Susan's parents are less than pleased with Michael who works in a hardware store as a floor clerk. He is essentially a jobler, doing little tasks around the store for its owner. He stocks shelves, mops floors, occasionally runs the cash register.

Michael and Susan marry secretly when she becomes pregnant with their only child, Judith. Michael is just 16 and she is only 15. After their marriage, Michael begins to stay away from home after work, leaving Susan to care for their infant daughter. Susan wonders where her husband spends his early evenings.

One night, Michael Lesser comes home reeking of bourbon. Susan smells this horrible odor. Her parents do not drink alcoholic beverages, so she doesn't recognize the smell on her husband's breath. Their young daughter Judith is in her wooden high chair; she bangs a spoon against the table. Michael reaches over and slaps his daughter. Susan stands in shock in her apron, holding a bowl of spaghetti in her hands. Tears form in her eyes, but she holds back. She places the warm bowl in the center of the table, ignoring Judith's sharp crying. Michael sits down across from his daughter, hangs his head.

"I've made spaghetti," Susan almost whispers. She sits down next to Judith's high chair, leans in close to her daughter, says quietly, "Shush now." Judith slowly stops crying, bangs her spoon tentatively against the table. Michael raises his head, glares at his wife. Susan takes the spoon from Judith who promptly cries again. Then, Michael is like a crazy man, jumping up from his chair which falls backwards from the force of his sudden rise. The chair clatters on the floorboards. He yells, the words incomprehensible to Susan. Michael's speech is so thick with alcohol that it does not make sense to her. Next, Michael picks up the plate in front of him on the table and tosses it toward Judith. The plate sails over the top of his little girl's head and crashes into the far wall, shattering into three large pieces. Susan is up, sheltering her child from her husband, a man she does not recognize.

Susan bravely says, "Stop it, Michael."

And he hits her across the back of her neck, so that she stumbles and falls onto Judith. The high chair rocks back, teeters for what seems an eternity to Susan, then rocks back down and stabilizes on its four legs. She pants, forces herself not to scream, not to cry out. Susan pulls Judith, who is strangely quiet, from the high chair. She heads toward the side door that leads onto the carport. She almost makes it across the kitchen; but she feels Michael's hand in her hair. He grabs so much of it that he brings her up short. Judith hangs limply in her arms.

"You can't leave me," Michael spits.

Susan deliberately relaxes; her terror so palpable she feels her heart will burst through her chest at any moment. She takes as deep as breath as she can, then lets it out forcefully. She goes as limp as her daughter, begins to crumple toward the kitchen floor. Michael goes down with her, collapses into tears. Susan holds Judith close against her shoulder; with her free hand, she gently rubs her husband's head which settles in her lap. Susan's tears also begin to flow; there is no stopping them. Her daughter is thankfully sound asleep.

By Judith's third birthday, Michael is a drunk.

9- DECEMBER AIR

Susan stands, leaves Michael weeping on the floor. She lifts Judith, bundles her daughter in a coat she takes from a hook by the back door. She puts on her own coat, takes the keys from the dish on the counter, opens the door and walks into the cold December air of West Virginia. Snowflakes fall through the night sky. Susan goes to the passenger side of the car, unlocks it, puts Judith in the used car seat she makes Michael purchase at the Salvation Army thrift store. She gently shuts the passenger door, walks around, climbs behind the wheel. As she begins to close the door to the car, Michael reaches in, grabs her wrist. He spits once more, "You can't leave me."

"Oh yes, I can Michael. I have to."

And she slams the door on his wrist, opens it again so he can pull his arm from where it is briefly pinned. As he clutches his arm to his chest and bends to yell, Susan starts the car and pushes the accelerator. The car lurches forward for a moment; she brakes hard, puts the transmission in reverse and pushes the accelerator again. The car lurches backward. Then, the tires skid briefly as she shifts from reverse into forward. Susan heads for her parents' home on the north side of Beckley. She does not bother to look back through the rearview mirror.

Her mother and father greet her at their door. Her father takes Judith into the upstairs bedroom, puts her down. She's sound asleep.

Susan's mother makes her daughter a cup of hot chocolate. They sit on the couch in the living room, and Mrs. Holmes holds Susan tightly by the shoulder. The hot chocolate sits on the coffee table, cooling. Her mother gently asks her what has happened. Susan tells her of Michael's drinking and a little bit about tonight's rage. Mrs. Holmes advises her daughter to hire a good lawyer and exit the marriage.

"You never wanted me to marry Michael in the first place."

"As I understand it," says her mother, "you didn't have a choice."

Susan stands abruptly, says, "Good night, mother."

"Good night, sweetheart."

The next morning despite the protests of her parents, Susan takes Judith and returns to Michael. She drives back to their house, parks their car, unlocks the side door, walks into the kitchen, starts the percolator which she always prepares for the next morning. She picks up the high chair, puts Judith in it. She looks around. At first, the house seems quiet. From the distant master bedroom, she thinks she hears Michael's snore. *He's probably passed out.* She turns to Judith, cheerily announces that it's time for oatmeal and raisins.

Five minutes later, Michael stumbles into the kitchen, crosses to Susan, kisses the back of her head and then her shoulder. "Hey honey." Susan turns, throws her arms around her husband's neck, kisses him full on the mouth. "Good morning, Michael. How'd you sleep?"

"Not bad, I guess." He looks around, bewildered. "Did you and Judith get up early or something?"

He doesn't remember. She smiles, "Yes, darling. Judith woke early. I think she's hungry. I'm making oatmeal. You want some?"

"Nah," he says. "I'll just have coffee. Is it ready?"

"Almost."

"Great." And Michael heads out of the kitchen, speaks over his shoulder. "I'll be right back; gonna take a quick shower."

"Sure thing, darling. I'll be here."

Michael stops at the doorframe, leans back into the space of the kitchen, smiles at his wife, and says, "That's swell, Susan. Thanks."

When he returns from his shower, he's dressed for the store. Susan comes close, straightens his thin black tie. She kisses him on the lips; he reciprocates. Susan puts her head on Michael's shoulder and closes her eyes. She imagines her cheek resting against God, who is as solid as her husband. She whispers, "I love You."

Michael responds, taking Susan's face in his large palms. He pushes his tongue into her mouth. When he pulls away, he continues to hold her face. Michael says, "I love you, too Susan." Then, he turns to the counter, picks up his coffee cup. "But, I gotta go to work now." He looks at Judith who is playing in her oatmeal with her hands. "Bye baby." Judith looks up at her father, goes back to the oatmeal. Michael makes the effort, comes close to his daughter. He pats her gently on top of her head, then kisses her there.

"See you later, Susan." Then, he goes out the door. He comes back almost immediately. "The car's locked. Where are the keys?"

"Here," says Susan pulling them from her skirt pocket. She hands them to her husband who takes them. He examines his wife, squeezes his eyes shut for a split second, thinks hard. *Why are my car keys in her pocket?* Then he dismisses his many and conflicting thoughts, and leaves.

Susan sits down across from Judith, puts her head in her arms she crosses on the table. She sighs. Judith bangs her spoon against wood. Susan raises her head, smiles at her young daughter. "Shush, sweetheart. Your daddy doesn't like that; he doesn't like that at all.

We're going to have to be careful, Judy baby. C[...]
squeals, bangs the spoon against the table. Susan[...]
snatches the utensil from her daughter's grip. "I said, w[...]
have to be careful, baby. And I mean careful." Susan cle[...]
teeth and puts the spoon under her right thigh. She puts h[...]
back down on the table, closes her eyes again as Judith begi[...]
scream for the missing toy.

10 - VIETNAM DARK

Rick comes to. He's on his back, stretched out on straw on a dirt floor. His ankles are bound together with leather thongs. His hands are free, but he realizes pretty quickly that his right arm is broken. He can make out the sky through narrow slats of the roof above him. He hears a scratching sound in the corner which is so dark he can't make out what is scratching. *Probably a rat.* He feels his forehead with his left hand; there's blood along the hair line. His tongue is dry, almost stuck to the roof of his mouth. He tries to roll over on his side to relieve pressure on his tailbone. The struggle is worth it; he winds up resting on his left shoulder and left hip with his knees bent. He tries to relax but he's in pain and he's hungry as well as thirsty. He notices he's crying. *What? Was I crying when I was unconscious? When did this start?* He reassures himself that anyone would cry given this amount of pain and uncertainty. He ignores his father's voice in his head: *You're a man; buck up!*

The scratching continues but the sound is moving along the far wall. *As long as it stays over there!* From his vantage point, Rick sees he's not alone. His co-pilot, Bob is seven or eight feet from him, stretched out on his stomach. He seems to be breathing but he's obviously not awake. Rick starts to speak, but feels a kick against his calf. Someone behind him whispers, "Don't. Be very quiet."

"Who's that?"

"Hunter," says Zach, who is the Huey's crew gunner.

"How many of us?"

"Four," says Zach. "We lost Angelo and Peters."

"Where are we?"

"No idea." Silence follows except for men breathing and that infernal scratching. Then Zach says, "I know the Viet Cong dragged the whole damn helicopter along with us. I know that much. And they've tortured poor Bob twice now."

"God," whispers Rick, a cold sweat beading up on his whole body. "How long have I been out?"

"About thirty-six hours."

"Shit," says Rick. He is surprised; swearing is not typical of him because his mother hates foul language. His father, on the other hand, is known for his obscenities, at least when Judith is not nearby.

"So, how long have we been here?"

"About twenty-four hours."

And these people have tortured one of us twice! The fear of dying which Rick experiences in his recurring dream suddenly changes to an intense terror. He begins to shake, sweat pouring off his body, soaking what's left of his uniform. "Oh God," he mumbles. "Oh God."

Zach chuckles softly behind him. "Yeah, He better help us because we're in the crapper!"

At that very moment, a lock clicks and two short men rush into the cell, pull Zach to his feet and begin to drag him away. Zach cries out in a loud voice, "Well, this is it boys. See you on the other side!" Rick notices there's no tremor, no sound of fear in the man's voice. *How is that possible?*

The two guards disappear with Zach Hunter in tow. He doesn't make it easy, dragging both his legs behind him, limp in their grip.

The lock clicks behind the three men. Two minutes later, Rick hears Zach's guttural scream, then a low groan, and total silence after one more hair-raising howl. Rick begins to cry. Bob stirs. Rick quiets himself, not willing to terrify his colleague. His co-pilot whispers, "Is that you, Rick?"

"Yes, it's me." Rick hears the tremor in his voice, takes a deep breath, tries to stop shaking.

"You okay?"

Rick laughs softly, "Yes, I am. What about you?"

"Oh, I've seen better days."

Rick wants to know, but he's afraid to ask.

"Those gooks are pretty tough on me," Bob offers.

Gooks. I hate that term.

"What did they do to you, Bob?"

Bob stretches out his left arm, shows his hand to Rick. Rick cringes. The nails are blackened; dried blood coats each fingertip. *Oh Jesus. Oh, oh.*

"Yeah, it's been pretty rough." And Rick hears the same tremor in Bob's voice that he hears in his own.

"You think we'll get out of this?" asks Rick.

Bob doesn't respond immediately, then he says quietly, "I doubt it."

The lock clicks again; the door opens. A taller man enters, walks quickly to Rick, grabs his right arm. The sharp pain goes through the broken bone up into Rick's neck, shoulder, face, head. He shrieks, struggles to get his feet to touch the ground as the man pulls him across the dark room to the door. Halfway to the entrance, Rick passes out.

When he comes to, he's seated in a wooden chair in the center of a cinderblock room; the floor beneath his feet is concrete. A drain is in the floor; water is running somewhere nearby. A bright light shines in his eyes. He hears a voice speaking English with only a slight accent. He can't make out what the voice is saying. Rick's right arm hangs limply from his side and is numb. His feet which were booted are now bare. This makes Rick very nervous. He sits for what seems like hours, waiting. Nothing happens. The light grows annoying; the sound of the water running even more disturbing because Rick is incredibly thirsty.

Suddenly, he speaks, "Hey!"

Nothing.

He yells again, "Hey! Hey! You can't just keep me in this chair forever, you know! Hey!"

The voice in the background speaking in English grows louder. Rick makes out a few words: "Your government has abandoned you. The people of America have forgotten you. No one is coming to help you." Then, the words fade before becoming very loud again. The message repeats, fades, repeats, gets louder each time.

A door at the far end of the room suddenly opens. A diminutive figure enters, dressed in a long black gown with a white sash above and around the waist. Odd looking sandals cover socked feet. Long hair flows from under a broad rimmed straw hat. As the figure comes closer, Rick recognizes a woman. She carries a small metal cup in her hands, which she brings to Rick's face. She offers the contents to his lips. At first, he resists until he realizes the cup contains water, cool and delightful. He drinks all of the offered liquid, approximately four ounces. *Not enough.*

He rasps, "Please, more."

She grins at him; her teeth are black. There's a fearful twinkling in her eyes which are also pitch black. She speaks with a thick accent, "No more for you." She turns and slowly walks to the door, exits, disappears into the dark outer area Rick glimpses for a moment before the door is shut.

Several hours later, two men enter from the same door, untie Rick from the chair and drag him back to the original cell. No other prisoner is there. Rick barks, "Where's my co-pilot? What have you done with Bob? Where's Bob?" The two men ignore him, turn and walk out of the room. The lock clicks.

Rick's right arm is swollen especially at the shoulder, the elbow, the wrist and is completely useless. He pushes off with his left arm, and manages to sit up. He scoots until he is able to lean his back against a wall. He sighs, closes his eyes, tries to sleep. *Bob. Hope you're still with us.* Then, Rick thinks of Charlie. *Oh Charlie, are you all right?*

11 - STRAIGHT "A"

Annabelle watches *Tom and Jerry* cartoons in the afternoons after school while doing her arithmetic homework or studying reading and writing. Turtle Creek Township's public schools are adequate, or so her mother and father tell her. She doesn't know if they are trying to convince her or themselves. *Who can afford private school anyway?* School is fun. Annabelle especially likes jumping on the trampoline or playing soccer in Physical Education, but hates taking public showers. *Who doesn't?*

Annabelle is a straight "A" student, and at the top of her small class. She excels in her science coursework and in mathematics. Her brother, Charlie is a solid "B" student and barely in the top half of his even smaller class. He excels in baseball. Essentially, all Charlie is interested in is baseball, and within baseball his interest is even narrower - his full passion is to become the best baseball catcher possible. He plans to play for the Cincinnati Reds.

Annabelle, even at her young age, has her own ambition. She's not shared it with anyone except her brother Charlie, who she loves dearly. One evening while star-gazing in their front yard, she confides in him. She says, "I know what I want to do when I grow up."

He laughs. "What's that, Annie-belle?"

She looks around as if her secret must not escape. She hesitates. "I want to be a doctor, Charlie. A baby doctor."

"A baby doctor?"

"You know," she whispers, "a pediatrician."

Charlie's embarrassed. He's not sure what a pediatrician does. "You mean, you want to deliver babies? Help mothers have babies?"

"No silly," she grins. "I don't want to help mothers have their babies. I want to help their children grow up healthy."

"Oh," says Charlie. *I get it now. I remember a pediatrician stitched up your hand, Annie. I remember.*

Their brother, Rick wants to be a long haul, over the road truck driver. Always makes Charlie smirk when he thinks of his big brother behind the wheel of a giant semi. Given Rick's skill fixing engines, Charlie thinks Rick ought to be an auto mechanic or an engineer. But, Rick tells him, "No, Charlie. I want to drive trucks across country. All through the night, I want to be on the road. I want to see the world."

"From a truck cab?"

"Sure. Why not?"

Charlie thinks of all sorts of reasons, but holds his tongue.

Rick and Charlie sit on the steps that lead up to the front porch. Charlie turns to Rick, "I want to see the world, too."

Rick smiles, says, "Well of course you do. And you will. You know Charlie you're going to travel more than I am. And certainly more than Annabelle. Once you're catching for the Big Red Machine, you're going to get to go all over the place."

Charlie imagines squatting behind home plate at Riverfront Stadium in Cincinnati. *Wow!*

While Charlie daydreams, Jim comes from inside the house. He stands behind his sons. Suddenly, Charlie feels a hard blow to the back of his head. He doesn't know what's happened, but he falls forward toward the bottom of the short group of stone steps. He lands face forward on the sidewalk. His nose bleeds. He has a sharp headache. He hears his father behind him, screaming something. Rick bends close to his face. "You okay?" Then, Charlie hears Rick argue with their father. Charlie can't make out what either of them says. Their words are muffled like they are spoken through gauze. Charlie stays where he is; allows the blood to seep out of his nose onto the sidewalk. He listens. The muffled voices continue, get very loud then quiet again.

Rick comes back, close to his face. "Charlie? Charlie?"

"Huh?"

"Can you get up?"

"I don't know."

Charlie hears the front door slam. He asks, "What happened?"

Rick shakes his head. "Dad is mad cause you forgot to take out the trash, and he says you left the light on in the upstairs bathroom."

"Oh," says Charlie. *Now I get it.* He looks at Rick, slowly sits up, holding his hand against his nose which continues to bleed a little. "What did he do? Kick me?"

"Yes, he did. Just kicked you right in the back of your head."

"Yeah," laughs Charlie, wincing. "That's what it feels like."

Rick helps Charlie to his feet. "Let's go inside; put some ice on it."

"Sure thing," says Charlie. As he stands, he leans over and vomits into the grass. "Oh, sorry Rick."

"No, that's okay."

12 - ENDLESS DAY

Rick wakes with a start. Behind the wall he hears moans, and what he imagines are blows to the body. The sounds go on and on and on until all is silent. Bob never returns to the common cell. Zach is thrown back in the same manner a sloppy fisherman might toss back an unwanted fish; he smacks the floor and remains in a heap through the night. When he wakes, Zach warns, "We won't be together much longer, Rick. Soon, the gooks will separate us."

Rick nods. *Of this I'm certain. Zach's right. Being with another person is so - so good. So good.*

Sure enough, the next morning before dawn, the same two soldiers come through the one door; grab Zach and drag him off. Rick is alone. Somewhere, so is Zach. So is Paul, who is the remaining man of Rick's helicopter crew. They are each alone except for his co-pilot who must be dead. *They beat him to death.* The familiar cold sweat pours from under Rick's arms, and between his legs. He shakes it off. He bites his bottom lip until it bleeds slightly; he tastes the blood. *I'm not doing this. I'm not going to melt down. Name. Rank. Serial Number.*

He spends this second day exploring the small space. In the far corner, he finds a bucket. He knows this is his toilet. As he lifts the lid, he feels the first drop of rain through the narrow roof slats. Then, the rain comes down harder; soon the floor turns to mud. Rick sits in one of the corners with his left arm bundled around his knees which he pulls up to his chest. His swollen right arm hangs limply at his side. In his mind, he begins to take apart his father's Chevy truck, piece by piece. He removes the tires, the wheels, the axle, the drivetrain, the transmission. Then he dismantles the engine, part by part. Finally, he breaks down the body of the truck until the whole machine is arranged on the ground in front of him. Next, he examines each piece for defects. Eventually, he puts the whole Chevy back together. He sighs. *Nice job there, Rick. Nice job.*

Food arrives through a small window at the bottom of the door. *I've seen this in some movie. The Man in the Iron Mask?* He stands up, stiff. He walks over to the door, sits right beside the small bucket with a wooden lid across its top. He's wary. He lifts the lid; inside is a small amount of something grey and mushy in appearance. He has no idea. There's no utensil. At the bottom of the bucket, beside the mush, is a tiny cup of tea or what Rick assumes is tea. Steam rises from it. The mush that he takes in his fingers is lukewarm; salty to his tongue and not entirely unpleasant to swallow. The hot tea is weak, but delicious nonetheless. He's so hungry and thirsty; he could care less what the food and drink taste like. He eats and drinks everything. Then uses the bucket toilet. The day stretches into night. Rick curls up on his left side on muddy straw, and sleeps. In the morning, the bucket toilet is empty. No food appears until late in the afternoon; and it is the same as yesterday.

Three days later, Rick's arm remains swollen. Now the elbow is red and tender, and hot to touch. *That's an infection. I'm in trouble.* That afternoon, when the little door opens for food delivery, Rick shouts, "Doctor. Hey. I need a doctor for my arm."

A woman's voice comes through the door, "No doctor for you." Rick imagines the black eyes of the woman who gives him water that first day. This is the same one.

"Doctor. Or I'm going to die."

"You die then," says the voice.

Rick laughs. *Okay. Okay, I die then.*

But the next morning, the lock clicks and the wooden door opens to reveal a man with a white coat. He comes to Rick, picks up the limp, red right arm and turns it slightly. Rick faints.

When he wakes, several small black leeches are attached to his arm at the elbow. He shudders, screams, starts to pull at one. The lock clicks. A soldier enters, smacks Rick's left hand with a bamboo stick, yells, "No!" Rick looks at the man, stricken with his own disgust. But, he leaves the leeches in place. The next day, the man in the white coat returns, lifts Rick's right arm. Rick faints with the intense pain. When he awakens, he's in a bed and his arm is wrapped in white cloth strips. He prays no leeches lurk beneath.

A nurse sits next to him; she's young and pretty. From under a white cap, her black hair is straight and heavy, and rests squarely on her shoulders. Her teeth are straight although slightly yellow. Her skin is smooth; her eyes black. Rick smiles at her; she turns her head away and lowers her eyes. Then, she looks back at him, lifts him with her left arm behind his shoulders and offers him soup from a bowl. He sips it. Whatever it is, he loves it. He takes all she offers. Next, she gives him water from a larger cup than he's seen since the Huey helicopter falls out of the sky.

He rasps, "Thank you."

She only looks at him, apparently unable to understand his English. Rick smiles at her broadly. She again turns her head away and closes her eyes.

"You're very kind," he says.

She only looks again at him. He hands her the cup and gestures for more by cupping his hand and bringing it to his mouth. She smiles, turns, picks up a pitcher from the floor, pours water into the cup and offers it to Rick. He drinks all the water. He belches, says, "Oh, excuse me."

The young woman appears puzzled, shakes her head.

"Oh, I know you don't understand me, but I haven't spoken to anyone, any woman in so long, I just want to talk. I don't mind that you don't know what I'm saying. I don't mind at all."

The young nurse smiles.

A man appears at Rick's bedside. Using perfect English, he barks at him, "Shut up."

Rick glances at the man, who is taller than any of the other Viet Cong he's met. He ventures, "Why should I?" Of course, the man smacks Rick in the jaw with his fist, then says, "Answer your question?" Rick rubs his face, and nods. The man sits on a wooden stool next to the bed. "No one here is going to help you."

Rick tries not to look at the young woman who stops her smile and seems frozen in place. The man glances at the young woman, says, "She's not here for you. She's here to do what I tell her to do." The man then speaks roughly to the young nurse. She looks down and bows her head repeatedly.

Rick also nods his head once.

The soldier ignores the young nurse, addresses Rick, "You were on a bomb run, weren't you? You and your crew were planning to bomb Hanoi."

Rick gives the man his name, his rank, and his serial number.

"But you failed. You failed to reach your target. You're a failure." The man rocks the stool back slightly, folds his arms. "Why did you try to bomb Hanoi?"

Again, Rick gives the man his name, his rank, and his serial number.

13 - NOT READY

Susan pulls the spoon from beneath her thigh and gives it back to Judith who squeals with delight, bangs it on the table. Susan laughs.

"I guess that's the way it's gonna be."

She takes the half-eaten oatmeal from Judith, and scrapes it into the trash can under the sink; she washes the bowl and puts it in the dish drainer. Judith keeps banging the spoon on the table.

"As long as your father isn't here, honey, bang away."

Susan begins to sing; she sings a lullaby her mother sings to her when she is little: *You are my sunshine, my only sunshine; you make me happy when skies are grey; you'll never know, dear how much I love you. Please don't take my sunshine away. The other night dear as I lay sleeping, I dreamed I held you in my arms; when I awoke dear I was mistaken; so, I hung my head and cried.*

Finally, Judith drops the spoon which clangs against the linoleum floor. Instead of crying, Judith lifts her arms toward her mother and mumbles an approximation of "up." Susan dries her hands, picks up her daughter. "Let's go to the park, okay? We'll take a bath, get dressed, and go to the park."

The park is public, and not far from the house. Susan bathes and dresses Judith; they walk to the park with Susan pushing Judith seated in the cheap cloth stroller bought at the Salvation Army thrift store at the same time the car seat is purchased. At the park, Susan pushes Judith in a wooden baby swing consisting of a box with a seat and a gate with a leather strap between the legs. The swing teeters when pushed so that Judith feels like she's twisting through the air. She squeals with delight. Everything is wonderful here in the park.

Later, Susan drops off her daughter at the Methodist church where several other children are kept by volunteer church women so that local members who must are able to work in order to put food on their tables. Judith is put in a crib and allowed to cry most of the afternoon. Susan doesn't know. And it's not that the church women don't care; it's just the way children are meant to be treated. The lady who runs the volunteer childcare center thinks: *Let them cry; they'll go to sleep eventually.* And eventually, Judith does sleep from exhaustion. There are only so many tears to cry.

Susan continues to work part-time but no longer at the same restaurant where she meets Michael. Soon after their marriage, she moves up to a classier diner where her tips are better. Susan excels at The Chart restaurant as she proves she is an attentive and caring waitress. The food, luckily, is excellent too. In addition, the owners are kind; they accept that Susan can't work full-time with a young one at home. Susan works twenty to twenty-five hours a week for the couple who owns The Chart Restaurant and Bar.

Often, Judith stays with her grandmother, Alena Holmes at the Holmes' house in north Beckley because the Methodist church volunteer women prefer not to work at night. Many times, the owners of The Chart need Susan in the evenings. Susan calls her mother who always says, "Well of course darling. Just bring her over."

Judith loves Granny Holmes, who plies her with candy, picture books and pretty new clothes. At Granny and Grandpa Holmes' house, she's never left in a crib to cry. Granny Holmes rocks her to sleep before putting her down. She always gets a bottle, too. Like the public park, the Holmes' house is a wonderful place for Judith.

Mr. Holmes is a kind man who loves his wife, his daughter and his granddaughter. He doesn't care much for his son-in-law but he's civil to Michael. Whenever Judith is at his house, Grandpa Holmes makes certain he spends some special time with his little angel grandchild. He makes Judith a wooden puppet shaped like a very tall girl with strings attached from its joints to a cross stick. Joel Holmes creates a beautiful marionette but Judith is too young to understand its use. Susan puts it high up on a shelf in a closet at home so that Judith only sees the puppet once. Grandpa Holmes makes her a top instead. Judith can't make it spin by herself but she enjoys it when Grandpa Holmes makes it spin across the wooden floor in their den. Joel doesn't fully comprehend why the marionette should be any different. Surely Susan and Michael might operate the puppet for Judith's pleasure. *Ah well, to each his own, I guess.*

Mrs. Holmes is a kind woman who loves her husband, her daughter and her granddaughter. Besides buying Judith candy, picture books and pretty new clothes, Alena enjoys taking her granddaughter to the Beckley YWCA swimming pool. She insists Judith learn to swim even as a toddler. Susan is horrified, but allows it because she trusts her mother. *Nothing bad is going to happen. Nothing bad.*

Alena takes Judith into the shallow end of the pool, holds her carefully by the chest up close to her arms. Judith squeals, kicks the water, laughs. Alena quickly dunks Judith under the water, brings her right back up. Judith sputters, looks wide-eyed at her Granny Holmes. Alena repeats the process. Judith starts to cry, but Alena says, "Ah, ah. No, no." Then, dunks Judith once more. Once again, Judith's face pouts and tears begin. "No, no Judy. Again?" Judith shakes her head adamantly. "Come on, baby. You can do it." And with those words, Alena quickly dunks Judith again. This time Judith struggles under the water, kicks violently. At the same time, she tries to bite her grandmother's arm. When Alena brings her back up from underneath the water, Judith is already crying. She screams. People around the pool turn to look. Alena is embarrassed. She shakes Judith once, then stops. "I'm sorry Judy. Granny won't do that again. I'm sorry." She steps out of the shallow end and wraps Judith into a large towel, holds her close to her body, rocks her gently. "You aren't ready for such an adventure, are you baby?"

Judith looks right into Alena's eyes and clearly says, "No, not ready."

14 - BLOCKING BLOWS

Rick puts his hand on his father's shoulder. Jim turns. Rick says, "You shouldn't treat Charlie that way."

Jim glances at Charlie who is stretched on the couch in the other room, his head back, tissue paper to his nose. "I can treat your brother however I see fit, Richard."

Rick shakes his head, "Well, you just shouldn't kick him in the back of the head. It's not fair. He didn't even see you coming."

"I don't care about fair. I care about making him do the right things in life."

That's not going to do it, Dad. Don't you know that? Instead Rick tries, "I want him to do the right things too Dad. But I don't think kicking him down the front steps is going to do the trick, do you?"

Jim's face twists. He raises his right arm, but Rick blocks the blow with his own left. A right cross to his father's jawbone would do. But, he restrains himself. He blocks the blow instead, then walks through the front door and out into the yard. He stands there, looking at the clouds in the sky. He sees a little rabbit shape; the rabbit appears to hop across the expanse of blue sky from wisp to wisp of white cloud. *I wish I could run away like that. I'd take Annabelle and Charles with me.*

Rick waits fifteen minutes before re-entering the house. Charlie is on the couch, still holds tissue paper against his nose. "Hasn't it stopped bleeding yet, Charlie?"

"Oh probably," answers Charlie. "I'm laying low."

Rick laughs. "Yeah, I don't blame you."

"Where is he?"

"Dad? Oh I don't know. Upstairs probably. Maybe in the garage."

Charlie sits up. "I've got to figure out some way to keep out of his reach."

"That's hard, Charlie. After all, you didn't even see him coming. Neither did I." *Dad's unpredictable. Sometimes he's fine; other times he's crazy mad.*

Charlie seems to read Rick's mind. "Yeah, he's kind of hard to predict, isn't he?"

"I think maybe you try too hard to please him," ventures Rick.

"You think!" says Charlie.

Rick smiles. "Come on, I'll buy you a coke."

Charlie shakes his head. "No, I think I'll go to bed. I'm really tired." He stands, wobbles, catches his balance before completely losing it. He reaches out, touches Rick's shoulder to steady himself. "I'm okay. I'm just really tired."

"Yeah, okay. I'll tell Mom you won't be at dinner. You know how she is."

Every day of every week, Judith prepares dinner for 6 p.m. sharp. She sets the table for five people, expecting everyone to come to eat together as a family. When Rick tells her Charlie won't be at the table, she protests. She goes upstairs, knocks at her son's door. "Charlie?"

From behind the door, a muffled voice: "Yes, ma'am?"

"I want you at dinner."

"Yes, ma'am."

Judith turns from the door, satisfied. She goes back to the kitchen and tells Rick he is mistaken. "Your brother's coming to dinner."

"Okay."

Judith gives him a disapproving look, says: "Okay?"

"I mean, yes ma'am."

"That's better."

Rick opens the refrigerator to get the ice trays; he puts ice into each of the five glasses on the table. He refills the trays, putting them back in the freezer.

Judith says, "We'll have iced tea. It's on the second shelf."

Rick nods, opens the refrigerator again, finds the pitcher filled with tea, pours the drink into each glass, returns the container to the shelf.

Ten minutes later, Charlie appears in the kitchen doorway. His nose is not bleeding, but a large bruise has formed along its side and along his left cheekbone.

Judith exclaims, "My God, Charles. What happened to you?"

Before Rick can speak on his behalf, Charlie says, "Oh, it's nothing really, Mom. I tripped on the front steps and landed on the sidewalk. Right on my nose!"

15 - YOUNG NURSE

Rick remains in the hospital a few days. Those days are the most comfortable he has during his stint as a prisoner of war. He gets two meals a day, and water whenever he asks the nurse for it. His arm is set apparently while he is unconscious; the cast is a little soft he thinks, but at least he is not in pain. Now he's certain no leeches lurk under the cast.

The pretty nurse continues to comfort him in ways he never imagined he would appreciate. Little things make such a difference for Rick. This delicate young woman fluffs his pillow the first night, and he cries at such a simple display of tenderness. She offers him a piece of fruit he does not recognize, but which tastes tart and sweet simultaneously. She massages his bruised, sore feet with her tiny, rough hands. She washes his filthy hair, and picks the lice from it. She shaves his unruly beard and mustache. She even brushes his teeth. He is so grateful only tears come. During the kindnesses of this lovely nurse, Rick discovers how terribly he misses his mother.

On the fourth day in the hospital, Rick tries to get out of the bed. When he swings his legs over the edge, five soldiers rush to his location, guns raised at his head and cocked, ready to be fired. He puts his hands up instinctively, and swings his legs back into the bed. "Easy, easy guys. I'm not going anywhere." The men hold their stance, keeping their guns aimed at him. Rick decides to lie down. When he does, the soldiers slowly lower their rifles and begin to walk away. When Rick looks at his nurse, he sees she's crying. "Oh, it's okay. Sweetheart, don't cry." She just stares at him, then puts her head on his shoulder. He touches her black hair. Apparently one of the soldiers notices because he starts back to Rick. The soldier puts his bayonet on the end of his weapon as he moves closer. When he gets to the bed, he thrusts his rifle in Rick's direction. The young nurse stands up, screams. As she does, Rick realizes he's in great danger of being skewered. He blocks the oncoming thrust of the bayonet with the cast on his right arm, then raises his arms again. He yells, "No, don't."

The bayonet comes at him anyway. It pierces his right shoulder; dark, almost black blood spurts as the soldier pulls the bayonet out to strike a second time. The young nurse leaps in front of Rick, shielding him from the bayonet which almost strikes her back. But the soldier reacts, halts his thrust. He speaks roughly to the young woman, tries to move her. But she's determined. She grabs onto Rick's neck and does not let go.

The soldier gives up, moves away. When Rick gets the woman to release him, he sees dark blood on her face. *That's mine, I think.* He tries to ask her if she's okay, if she's been struck but he doesn't know how. The nurse begins to examine him. She rises, gathers supplies, comes close to him, pulls away the remains of his shirt which is blood-soaked. The wound is small; she cleans it out, rubs some sort of ointment well into it, making it sting first then burn. Then she wraps a long strip of gauze around his shoulder and neck so as to cover the injury. She gives him a bitter drink. Within a few minutes, Rick grows drowsy. He tries to relax, but his mind fights sleep. He takes the young woman's hand and squeezes, then succumbs to unconsciousness.

When Rick wakes, the rest of the hospital is still. The young nurse is no longer at bedside. Rick figures the soldiers stand guard in the hallway just outside the door to this ward. Rick wonders what place in northern Vietnam this hospital serves. *Wonder if I'm in Hanoi.* He realizes he'll likely never know. He tries to go back to sleep, but he's thirsty. On the table beside the bed is an empty cup; on the floor is the pitcher. He reaches over the side of the bed, picks up the pitcher with his left hand, pours water into the cup, and drinks. Sleep comes soon after.

In the morning, the soldiers take him back to his cell. As the lock clicks, Rick scoots his back against a wall and looks up through the roof slats to a distant sky. He is able to see a single brilliant star. He thinks of the pretty young nurse, of her kindnesses. *I'll never see her again.* He cries softly, exactly like a man.

16 - TREE FARM

Charlie and Annabelle cook together in the six months after Rick's disappearance in Vietnam. Annie does the actual cooking; and Charlie helps as much as he is able. Judith spends most of her time in bed in alternating states of shock and mourning. Jim goes to work, comes home, eats, sits in the den, reads his newspaper, then watches a little television and retreats to the bedroom with Judith. Charlie and Annie keep each other company through these long months. Each wears a copper bracelet with "Richard Lewis Logan: KIA" etched across its surface. Charlie only takes his off when he plays baseball. Annie never removes hers so that below her 'killed in action' bracelet, her skin displays a slight green tinge.

Christmas season arrives. Jim refuses to drive out into the country as they usually do to pick and cut a fresh tree. Charlie is capable of driving although not legally, having failed Driver's Education last spring. But he talks Annie into going with him anyway. He steals the Chevy keys; and early Saturday he and Annie climb into the cab of the truck, start it, slowly back out of the driveway and sneak off. The roads are clear for which Charlie is grateful. He drives too slowly; drivers behind him lay on their horns and try to pass his truck whenever they can. Since this is an early Saturday morning, these bullying drivers are far and few between; again Charlie and Annie are grateful.

The drive to the Christmas tree farm is long. Annie functions as navigator, holding the map of Ohio in her lap.

"Turn at the next light, Charlie."

"Left or right," he asks his little sister.

"Oh, turn right."

Charlie flicks on the turn signal, slows, and makes a nice right turn onto the country road. They travel twenty-five miles before Annie says, "Okay, we're coming up on the road we need to turn onto. It's gonna be a left, Charlie."

"Okay, just let me know."

He continues for another fifty yards or so when Annie yells, "There it is! Right there!"

Charlie brakes briefly but realizes he's overshot the turn.

"You missed it!"

"Yeah, we'll have to turn around somewhere along here and go back."

"Okay."

"Keep your eyes open for an easy turnaround."

They travel another hundred yards or so when Charlie sees a driveway leading to a farm. The entrance is on his right which he likes. He turns in, stops. *Damn, I've got to back up onto the road!* He puts the truck in reverse and starts to back up. Annie yells, "Don't do that, Charlie. That's so dumb!"

"Well, what do you want me to do?"

"Go on up to the house. I can see a circle that will turn you around the right way."

"Okay." And Charlie puts the truck into forward and gives it gasoline. The truck bumps along as the driveway is dirt and rutted deeply here and there. As they approach the house, the front door opens, then the screen door, and a man in coveralls comes out on the porch.

"Oh shit!" says Charlie.

Annie looks. The man has a shotgun resting in the crook of his arm. He hasn't raised the rifle yet, but he appears to be ready to do so. Annie cranks down her window and calls out, "Sorry sir! We're just turning around. We're so sorry." About the same time, Charlie gives the truck more gasoline so that the tires kick up dust. The dust forms a thick cloud between them and the man on the front porch. He raises the shotgun. Charlie guns the truck, peels out, and moves it as quickly as he can down the bumpy driveway out to the country road. He barely stops at the entrance before making the left turn. In the rearview mirror he sees the man, small now, bending over, apparently laughing his head off.

The Chevy moves down the country road to the turn they missed. Charlie turns right. They travel another five miles before they reach Mike's Magical Christmas Tree farm. When Charlie gets out of the truck, his knees are like jelly. He bends over, and takes a deep breath.

"You okay?" asks Annie.

"Yeah," he says. "Let's pick out the best tree ever. Okay?"

"Sure thing!"

The couple who owns the Christmas tree farm reluctantly gives Charlie an axe. The wind is picking up as Charlie and Annie start their walk up and down the rows of trees. They take their time, eventually find several trees they like. Still they keep going. About forty-five minutes into the hunt, Annie finds the perfect tree.

"This is the one, Charlie."

Charlie stares at the tree. Annie watches her brother, who does not move. Annie touches his shoulder, says, "Charlie?"

Charlie seems to startle; he glances at Annie. "What?"

Annie repeats, "This is the tree, Charlie." She points to the beautiful specimen in front of her brother who nods. He examines the tree which is seven feet and perfectly "A" shaped with long needles. *Not a branch out of place; not one gap. A perfect pine tree for the living room.*

"You're right, Annie. Let's cut it down."

After Charlie chops the tree trunk to the proper spot, the tree falls. Annie puts on her leather gloves, hands Charlie his pair. Together, they pull the tree back to the Chevy. The man helps Charlie pick it up and put it in the truck bed.

"That's fifteen dollars."

Charlie pulls his wallet from his back pocket, hands the man a crisp ten and a crisp five.

Annie's very excited all the way home. Charlie begins to get a tight spot in his abdomen as he imagines their father's reaction to having his truck stolen and his children disappear for most of a Saturday.

Their father waits for them on the couch. When Annie enters through the front door, he says, "Your mother's asking for you. Upstairs, Annabelle."

The tone of voice impresses Annie. She says, "Yes sir." She heads up the stairs to her parents' bedroom. She knocks. From inside the room, her mother invites her to enter. Annie opens the door and steps into the dim room. Her mother is propped up in the bed with several pillows behind her shoulders.

"Come over here, Annabelle. Let me see you."

Annie climbs into the bed and sits where her mother gestures. Her mother's skin is pale and her hair dull. But her eyes are bright.

Her mother asks, "How are you, Annabelle? How's school?"

"School's fine, Mom."

"Good," says her mother. Then, Judith asks, "You're keeping your grades up?"

"Yes ma'am," says Annabelle.

"Good," repeats her mother.

Annie waits, then says, "I wish you weren't so sad, Mommy."

Judith smiles, whispers, "Don't worry about me, Annabelle."

Downstairs, Jim waits for Charlie to come in. A knock at the door, then Charlie's voice, "Hey Annie. Can you open the door? Remember, I'm dragging a tree!"

Jim walks to the front door, opens it to see his son pulling a large pine tree up the front steps to the porch.

Charlie looks up. He takes a deep breath, smiles. "Hey Dad. Look what Annie and I found. A real Christmas tree."

"You stole my truck," says Jim.

"Yes sir, I borrowed the Chevy." Charlie is stuck on the lowest of the four steps to the porch. His father stands on the top step, looking down on his son. The tree is heavy even though most of its bulk is resting on the sidewalk behind Charlie.

"You stole my truck," repeats his father.

Charlie decides to confess. "Yes, sir. I took your truck without your permission."

"You stole my truck, and you don't have a driver's license. You failed Driver's Ed as I recall."

"Yes, sir. I failed Driver's Education."

"You drove illegally and with your little sister."

"Yes sir; I did."

Jim waits, but his son doesn't add an apology.

Charlie explains, "Annie wanted a Christmas tree; so did I. You didn't want to buy one, so I promised Annie we'd find one. I realized on Friday that I'd need to drive out into the country to get the - "

Jim lurches down the three steps toward Charlie. He raises his right arm and strikes. Charlie drops the tree, and blocks his father's blow just as Rick once does. "No," he says, "No, you are not hitting me again."

Jim takes his right arm back to try again, and again Charlie blocks the strike. He repeats, "No Dad. No, you are not hitting me again."

Jim pants. He stands on the third step, and tries once more to hit Charlie. Again, Charlie blocks his father's movement. Jim drops his arm, sits down on the steps. To Charlie, his father appears dejected as if he's lost more than a battle with a son.

Charlie picks up the tree trunk. "You want to help me now?"

Jim glances up, shakes his head.

"Okay then," says Charlie. "Will you at least move out of my way so I can get the tree into the house? Annie and I want to decorate it tomorrow morning so it's ready for Christmas on Monday."

Jim scoots over to the far side of the step he's on. Charlie says, "Be careful now. These branches are really long and full so you're liable to get scratched."

Jim stands up, walks around Charlie and down the sidewalk to the street. He turns to the right and walks away. Charlie starts to call after his father, but thinks better of it. Instead, he drags the Christmas tree up the steps and into the foyer. He puts it down, calls upstairs, "Hey Annie. Annie-belle, can you come help me with this?"

A door opens, and Annie yells down, "Sure thing. I'm coming."

She comes down the stairs, stops.

Charlie says, "I'm going out to the garage to get the tree stand. Why don't you go back upstairs, ask Mom where in the attic the decorations might be."

"No," says Annie. "I want to surprise her." Annie's face brightens. "I'll climb up into the attic and find them. Okay?"

"Okay," says Charlie. "I'd like us to surprise Mom. That's a great idea, Annie."

Charlie walks out back to the garage. He stands outside the large double door. Snow begins to fall, slowly at first. When he opens the side door, Charlie notices a slight collection of snow - perhaps as much as a quarter of an inch - on the walkway around his feet. *Odd, I don't remember that dusting.* He enters the garage, locates the tree stand leaning against the far wall, grabs it, takes it back into the house where he sets it up in the front corner of the living room.

Annie comes in a few minutes later. She has two medium-sized boxes in hand. "There's a large one, too. I couldn't manage it on the attic steps."

"I'll get it," says Charlie. And he does.

17 - CHRISTMAS MORNING

Their mother, Judith comes out of her bedroom Christmas morning when she hears the song *O Tannenbaum* rising from downstairs. Annie screams, "It's Christmas! Mom! Dad! Christmas is here!"

Judith sits on the edge of the bed, finds her slippers underneath it, puts them on, goes into the bathroom to pee and brush her teeth and run a comb through her hair quickly. Her heart is doing little butterfly flutters; she's excited like she is when she is little and staying with Granny and Grandpa Holmes in north Beckley.

"I'm coming," she yells down to her children. She turns back to the bed. Jim stirs. "Get up, sleepyhead. It's Christmas." Jim groans, "All right. I'll be there. You go on."

With his permission, she almost stumbles down the stairs; she moves so fast. When she reaches the foyer, she turns. The Christmas tree greets her from the corner of the living room. A small fire is lit in the fireplace; it's not roaring yet, but soon it will be. The tree is bright and cheery, decorated with ornaments from the years of her marriage to Jim. Every year, at least one other ornament is added. Many years, she adds two or three to her collection.

"Oh, it's beautiful."

Charlie smiles. "Thanks Mom. Annie did most of the work."

Jim appears in the foyer at the foot of the staircase. Judith nearly skips over to him, giving her husband a big hug. "Oh Jim, thank you."

Her husband looks a tad bewildered, then winks at Charlie. He smooches with his wife briefly, says, "Well darling, you're welcome. But you really ought to thank our son. He's the one who got the tree this year. He and Annabelle picked it out."

Judith turns to Charlie. "Oh Charles; thanks honey. It's really a gorgeous tree."

Charlie says, "You're welcome Mom." And he makes an effort to smile at his father, who smiles in return.

Suddenly, Judith is in tears. She's not sobbing but the tears flow from both her eyes, down her cheeks. She stands there looking at the tree. *Oh Richard. Baby. Oh Rick.*

Charlie gets to her first, settles her on the couch. He commands Annie to get a cup of coffee for their mother, which Annie does. He holds his mother close. "What is it, Mom?" Jim sits on the other side of Judith, places his arm around her. He looks at Charlie and says, "Richard. It's Richard." And Judith breaks into sobs.

Charlie gradually starts to cry too. He realizes that Rick isn't coming home; he's not going to appear through the back door or the front door for Christmas. He isn't coming home at any time. Charlie cries when he first hears that Rick is missing in action in Vietnam; when Coach Coffey waves him over during afternoon practice to tell him his brother is most likely killed in action. But since that first day, Charlie is stoic, not crying except once or twice. Now, he shakes with the pain of this loss. *My brother. Oh, my brother - my best friend.*

Jim also begins to weep quietly; soon Annabelle sits at their feet and she cries, too. She shakes her head. *This is ridiculous. It's Christmas!*

She gets up, goes to the tree. "I'm playing Santa."

Judith wipes her eyes. She looks at Annie. She stammers, "Okay, Annie. Who's first?"

Annie reaches under the tree, pulls a beautifully wrapped red and green package with a large bow stuck on it; she reads the tag, "To: Judith; With Love: Jim. Here Mommy, it's for you from Daddy."

Judith unwraps the present; inside she finds a pink cardigan made of lambs' wool. "Oh Jim. It's so soft. Thank you, honey."

Jim hugs her. "You're welcome, darling." He looks at Annie. "Okay Santa. Who's next?"

Annie pulls another package from beneath the tree. She reads, "To: Charlie; From: Annie. Here Charlie. This one's yours."

Charlie opens the small gift. Inside he finds a pack of baseball cards. The cards represent the Cincinnati Reds' first string. "Oh thanks Annie." He gives her a kiss on her forehead. Charlie whispers, "Sorry Annie." She doesn't understand at first.

Annie, as Santa, continues to pick gifts from underneath the tree. Her mother gets another from her husband, a small bottle of Worth's *Je Reviens* cologne. Judith gives Jim a tie and a paperback book about growing houseplants. Annabelle opens a large package from her mother. The box contains a large obviously old, yet new appearing marionette. Annie looks at Judith with surprise. She is expecting a Barbie doll from her parents, so is simultaneously disappointed and thrilled. Judith says, "Your grandfather made her for me. I hope you like it." Annie puts the large puppet into the box, gives her mother a hug. She says, "Oh, thanks Mommy."

Annie returns to playing Santa, but finds no gifts under the tree from Charlie. She wonders briefly if Charlie has any of his allowance left after he buys the Christmas tree.

At last, Annie comes to the final package which is for Charlie. The card reads, "To: Charles; From: Dad." Charlie opens the box. Inside is a leather baseball glove. Charlie looks at his father, who is already in tears. Charlie rises from the couch, lets the glove drop. He walks to his father, puts his hands on the man's shoulders, guides him to his feet. Charlie hugs his father. "Thank you, Dad. Thank you so much."

18 - DROPPING OUT

In early March, Charlie abruptly drops out of high school. He doesn't recover from Rick's disappearance in Vietnam. Whereas Annabelle and Jim apparently recover, Charlie - along with his mother - begins to wallow in mourning. He misses Rick so much that he doesn't function well, especially at school. His teachers notice he's not paying attention. He misses classes, and he even begins to miss baseball practice. This alarms Coach Coffey, who calls Mr. Logan at work.

"I just wanted to let you know how worried I am about Charles."

Jim is nonchalant. "Okay."

"Charlie doesn't miss practice; that's not like him."

"Okay," repeats Jim.

"Well," says the coach. "I just wanted to let you know."

"Okay," says Jim once more.

The coach hangs up the phone, befuddled by Mr. Logan's lack of a reaction. This father's lack of concern bothers Coach Coffey so that he's now even more worried about Charlie.

Then, one afternoon the following week, he sees Charlie and Dave Pissleton coming out of The Talisman. Dave definitely looks tipsy, but Charlie doesn't. *What the hell are two kids doing in a bar?*

Charlie doesn't see his coach; neither does Dave. The two boys exit the tavern laughing. Dave slaps Charlie on the back, says, "So what'd ya think of your first beer? It was your first, wasn't it?"

"Yeah, sure. It was great."

Coach Coffey is across the street in the facade of a doorway. He watches Dave and Charlie move down the sidewalk. Dave's steps are wobbly, but Charlie could walk a straight line if he had to. The coach weighs his options, decides against confronting Charlie in Master Pissleton's company. Dave Pissleton has the reputation of being a troublemaker at the high school, and the coach doesn't know him personally. Dave doesn't play any sports. The coach is surprised to see these two young men together. What Coach Coffey doesn't know is that Charlie and Dave are neighbors, and see each other often although Charlie does not refer to Dave as a friend.

Dave sits on his porch. Charlie comes out the front door of his house and sits on his porch steps. The two houses are no more than eight feet apart. Dave yells over, "Hey there, Chuck."

"Hey Dave."

"Wanna do something?"

"Like what?"

"We could go sledding."

Charlie likes this idea immediately. He nods, says, "Sounds great. You got a sled?"

"Sure. Got a Red Flyer wooden sled for my birthday."

Turtle Creek Township sits on several hills just north of Cincinnati with a few great sled runs near their homes. Although it's March, snow remains on these hills.

Charlie yells, "I got to tell my mother."

Dave grimaces like Charlie is a toddler in his eyes. "Okay, whatever man."

"Be right back," says Charlie. He goes into the house, locates his boots, his gloves, his heavy winter coat, his knit cap. He swings by Annabelle's room; she's studying. He knocks gently on his mother's bedroom door.

"Yes?"

He cracks the door, says, "I'm going sledding with Dave from next door."

"Okay," she says. "Be careful."

"Yes ma'am."

The two boys pull the sled behind them to the top of Riker's hill, and go down the slope together. The wind is cold, and Charlie's fingers numb quickly as do his toes. After the fifth run, Dave pulls a small metal flask from inside his coat, takes a swig. The odor of rum lifts into the air around the boys, except Charlie doesn't recognize it. Dave offers, "This'll get you hot."

Charlie takes the flask, smells its contents. "Smells pretty nasty to me."

"Try it," says Dave.

Charlie takes a tiny sip; the liquid burns the tip of his tongue and he feels the fumes in his throat and nose as he swallows. He doesn't like it and gives the flask back to Dave. He says, "No thanks."

Dave laughs. "Suit yourself."

They take several more runs on Riker's hill, then head home.

After Spring break, Charlie attends school for a little more than three weeks; then he flunks a major test in his English Literature class, and afterwards breaks into tears in the boys' bathroom. At first, he stops going to that class in particular, then he avoids other classes in which he's having difficulty academically. Soon, he misses the pre-season baseball strategy sessions that Coach Coffey holds once a week after school. Then Charlie misses the first baseball practice session of the season. Finally he sleeps in, ignores his alarm clock, misses the school bus on the corner, does not attend any morning classes. He's called into the principal's office.

Mr. Morrison asks, "What's going on, Master Logan?"

"I'm dropping out of high school," says Charlie.

19 - THE HOTEL

Rick feels like his right arm inside the cast is rotting away. He can smell it sometimes at night but he's not certain; it may be in a dream that he smells that decaying odor. There's no pain coming from underneath the plaster, so he keeps his hope that his arm is healing. This hardly matters because the soldiers torture the rest of his body whenever they feel like it, which seems to be on a daily basis.

Rick misses the young nurse, especially during the long nights. He misses her black hair, her black eyes, her golden skin, the delicate touch she uses when she feeds him. He imagines her often, then drops into regret when he realizes she's not next to him.

He loses count of the days he's in captivity. He maintains a record at first, but once in the hospital, loses track. He thinks he's been a prisoner of war approximately a month or maybe two. Time is relative here. Some days are extraordinarily lengthy; others seem gratefully short. Rain is frequent so his clothes - what's left of them - are mildewed. His hair is matted to his scalp; lice run rampant. The scratching in the far corner - *got to be in the wall* - is continuous now.

The sound varies one morning. Rick hears a tapping on the wall rather than the scratching only, which is now in the background. The tapping is intermittent, sounds like it might be Morse code. *Must be Paul, or maybe Zach.*

He scoots over to the wall, leans in close, taps in a kind of shorthand: "Who?"

A short moment later, "Zach. Who?"

"Rick."

The tapping stops a few minutes, then comes in a flurry of one word comments and two word questions. Zach wants to know what happened, where's Rick been, who else is left, and so on.

Rick answers as best he can. He's not sure about Paul and says so. He knows Bob is gone; at least he's pretty sure.

Turns out Zach endures even more torture than Rick. Most of his fingernails are so seriously damaged from bamboo shoots being driven under them that Zach thinks he may lose his fingers if he survives his stay. Zach deliberately refers to his captivity as his "stay." Rick goes along with it. They come to name the prison "The Hotel."

When they are caught communicating through the walls, each is punished. Rick loses his food and water rations for two days; Zach reports his big toe on his left foot is smashed with a large hammer both of these two days. Rick wonders why Zach's punishment is so severe, although his own hunger is constant and scary to him. He fears starving to death. *Maybe I let on that I'm afraid of starvation.* The most effective torture is likely that which is tailored to the individual being tortured, he figures.

Rick imagines pitching a baseball to his little brother, Charlie. Charlie squats in the farthest corner of their back yard, mitt at the ready. Rick pitches a nasty fast ball which Charlie catches perfectly. Rick analyzes every motion of his own and of Charlie's. This eats up time, and distracts him from his hunger and thirst.

The next day, Rick and Zach communicate again. Rick is convinced this daily chatting keeps him sane. Without Zach's sense of humor and support, Rick is pretty certain he'd lose his ability to cope, and go directly off the deep end.

20 - SMALL ALLOWANCES

After he drops out of high school, Charlie sleeps a lot. Jim tries to get him out of bed, first by coaxing, then by threatening to kick him out of the house; but Judith refuses to allow this. Privately, she tells Jim that if Charlie goes, she goes. Jim isn't ready to chance losing his wife, so he tolerates his son's defiance. The most difficult part is to keep his anger under control. He begins to avoid his son.

Once he gets out of bed and begins to move, Charlie spends much of his time with his mother who remains less than herself. She is listless around the house, stays in her pajamas, housecoat and slippers until well into the afternoons. Charlie makes breakfast and lunch, and helps Annie with supper preparations. Judith uncharacteristically watches soap operas and situation comedies on the television in the den from late morning into late afternoon. Charlie cajoles his mother into dressing for dinner, so that Jim rarely sees Judith as she is most of the day. As far as her husband knows, *she's coming along.*

Jim takes her to the doctor after their immediate loss of Rick. The doctor examines Judith, tells Jim that his wife needs to cry more. Judith stares at Dr. Saunders and smiles. It's late February; Rick's Huey goes down and disappears in January. Not until Christmas morning, almost a year later, does Judith - along with Jim, Annabelle and Charlie - cry. Those tears kickstart Judith's recovery from crippling grief. By this time, however, Charlie drinks secretly, sometimes behind his own house with Dave providing the beer; other times, at the Talisman where the bartender, Joe doesn't bother to card him or ask him his age. Joe cares less. Charlie is a customer who spends his small allowance on alcohol. Charlie doesn't come home drunk. He drinks routinely but not excessively. The slight buzz he gets from the alcohol in beer - he only consumes beer, usually whatever is cheapest - numbs the pain of losing Rick. Charlie decides this pain can not be faced head-on. As his father avoids him, Charlie makes every effort to avoid this painful loss.

Over time, Charlie notices cravings he can't deny. If he can't find Dave who has no difficulty procuring beer, then he makes his way to the Talisman, where Joe is willing and even eager to sell Charlie beer. Joe does appear a bit concerned when Charlie starts to ask for two rather than one. He leans over the bar, asks, "So, what's with two, Chuckie?"

"Charlie."

"Whatever," says Joe. "Why you suddenly wanting two beers, man?"

"Cuz I like it."

This explanation apparently satisfies Joe, who sets the second draft on the bar in front of Charlie. Charlie sips it, savoring the flavor and the buzz.

When he comes out of the Talisman, Coach Coffey is on the sidewalk.

"Oh, hi Coach."

"Hello Charles." The man glances at the flashing sign over the bar. To Charlie, the coach appears to be thinking about a difficult problem. The large man shakes his head almost imperceptibly, then puts his big arm over Charlie's shoulder. "Charlie," he begins.

"Yes, sir?"

Coach Coffey continues, "I've got a scout coming next weekend from the Detroit Tigers' farm teams. I'd like you to come to practice, if you'd like."

Charlie is dumbfounded. *If I'd like?* He tells Coach that of course he'd like to come to practice. His surprise is all over his face.

The coach points to the Talisman, and adds, "And I don't want to see you coming out of here again."

Charlie promises.

21 - SLAP DOWN

Rick taps. Zach responds. Every day, Rick and Zach keep in touch. Later Zach tells how this communication keeps him alive. He tells the officer during his debriefing, "The gooks did everything in their power to keep us isolated from one another. Whenever they caught us talking, they slapped us down with penalties or tortures. But we were determined to keep our lines of communication open. Being able to share our daily trials and triumphs kept us from falling into utter despair."

Today, Rick taps out that he isn't able to keep any food down. He vomits everything he eats. "Luckily," he tells Zach, "I keep down water, what little I get."

Zach encourages Rick to keep eating anyway. "Don't let the gooks know you're losing everything. Keep eating. Dig a hole in the floor, hide your vomit."

Zach is right: *hard to know what the gooks are going to use against me.*

Rick eats the mush provided, but throws it up about five minutes after it hits his stomach. He does what Zach suggests; he digs a shallow hole and buries the mush he tosses up. He drinks all the water provided, and as usual this stays down. Rick sleeps as much as he can, whenever he can. When he's awake, he continues to imagine taking engines apart and putting them back together, the basics of changing the oil and the oil filter, how to change a tire, how to pitch a baseball. He also reviews pieces of information picked up in school: the Periodic Table of the Elements, formulas in algebra and geometry that he struggles to recall, the make-up of the atom, the location and names of countries, large and small, the constellations, their names and shapes and number of stars, and other tidbits. All of these mental exercises keep Rick from going berserk from the extreme boredom.

At the same time, these communications help Zach. Rick knows this is true because Zach has deep bouts of depression. Zach taps out his despair especially during dusk as the sun sets; a kind of down time to which Rick can not relate. Yet, Rick is perfectly willing to listen to Zach's long ramblings about how he wants this to end, how he desires death over this continued darkness, filth, boredom, pain. Rick tries to boost his companion's spirits; but it's not easy. Rick does his best to shield himself from Zach's negativity. *Keeping positive is key to my survival. And I am determined to outlast my enemies.*

Zach, however, in the mornings is relatively cheerful; taps out his gratitude to Rick for the help he gives the previous evenings.

"No problem," taps out Rick.

"Really man, you keep me alive."

Rick smiles. "My pleasure."

"Manage to keep supper down?"

"Nope," Rick taps back.

The lock clicks; Rick drops his hand to his side, closes his eyes quickly. The soldier runs to him, smacks him hard across the wrist with a bamboo stick, yells something incomprehensible to Rick even though Rick knows it is akin to a command not to communicate with his neighbor.

"Okay, okay all ready! I got it."

The soldier grabs Rick's shoulder, pushes him over onto the floor so that Rick is prone; the man shoves his boot into Rick's right shoulder blade and puts most of his weight on it. Rick cries out. The soldier seems to laugh, then jumps up and comes down on Rick's shoulder. Rick hears something inside snap. He faints from the momentary sharp pain. When he comes to, he is still on his stomach, dirt and straw in his mouth. He tries to move, but the pain in his upper back is excruciating.

Rick hasn't realized how much weight he's lost until he examines his right arm above the cast which no one has bothered to remove. He sees a gap between his arm and the cast and notices he can put several fingers between both. *I'm a rail.* He moves his shoulder gently; it's stiff and painful. He waits for his meal delivery, attempts to speak to the delivery person, "Hey, hey. I need to go back to the hospital." He gets no response. He knows to keep his shoulder moving; he gingerly rotates it slowly first in one direction, then in the other. He raises his arm hesitantly, lowers it. *If I don't keep it moving, my shoulder will freeze up on me.*

He tells Zach who encourages him. Together they face each long, usually uneventful, but always unpredictable day.

22 - SKIPPING STONES

Jim grows up in Aurora, Indiana along the Ohio River and not far from his eventual home, Turtle Creek Township across the border between the states of Indiana and Ohio. Aurora is a dirty little railroad town with a lumber mill on its outskirts where Jim's father, Peter James Logan grades lumber.

Jim is an only child and a lonely boy; he skips stones across the pond in the back half of his father's land and fishes there, too. He does these activities alone. He hooks the worms, casts the lines, brings in the fish, takes them off, cleans and fillets them, cooks them - all by himself. Before he comes into his father's house, he makes certain he always scrapes the mud from his shoes, leaves them outside. When he needs, Jim washes his clothes - all by himself.

Pete Logan usually comes home late as he stops by the local bar near the mill before managing the trip to his house. At night, Jim feeds himself, then does what little homework he has assigned from school while he listens to *The Shadow* on the radio. When he hears his father on the porch, before the man puts his hand to the door knob, Jim turns off the radio and heads to his room. Pete generally finds his son asleep or pretending to be asleep, his door closed and sometimes locked. Pete occasionally rattles the knob, but leaves his son alone. This man rarely worries or concerns himself with his boy.

Jim's mother, Elizabeth leaves when Jim is only a baby. As he grows older, he wonders why she doesn't take him along but when he is young, he doesn't think of her because he has no memory of her. Pete, his father, throws away all the crumpled black and white photographs of Elizabeth long before Jim is old enough to notice them. His father never mentions Elizabeth. Jim never learns why his mother leaves her husband or why she abandons her only child.

When his son is a baby, Pete Logan hires Miss Pattie Hogenbume, an older woman quite literally from the other side of the railroad tracks, to take care of him. She's kind, but almost deaf so sometimes she doesn't hear his soft voice or his insistent cry. He is ignored often. Dirty diapers are changed but infrequently; he's fed but not as often as his stomach demands. Miss Hogenbume cares for Jim until he is enrolled in kindergarten. Then she disappears. Jim doesn't know why she doesn't take him along with her when she leaves. He doesn't realize his father stops paying her or that this is the reason she goes on her way. Miss Hogenbume can't wait for Jim to come home from school. Mr. Logan opens his front door, and points. Miss Hogenbume walks away reluctantly. Jim cries himself to sleep because this woman - who is mother to him - is suddenly and inexplicably gone. He's only 5 years old.

School - a new and initially exciting experience - keeps him occupied. He loves math and art. Jim draws tiny stick men, gets in trouble with his teachers who scold him for using ink in the margins of his school's textbooks.

"These books are not yours, Master Logan."

"No ma'am."

"So, stop it." The teacher's face becomes red as a beet, and her voice is shrill.

Jim cries.

Pete notices this. His son cries about anything - a scolding, a skinned knee, a poke in the eye, thirst, hunger. *Stupid boy; stupid, sensitive boy.*

Jim is so shy; eventually he stops speaking to everyone except when he must speak. He talks in school only when the teachers call on him directly.

"Jim, what's the answer?" The teacher points to him.

"Huh?"

"The answer, Master Logan."

And then he tells the teacher the answer if he knows it. If he doesn't, he tells the teacher, "I don't know."

Jim takes long walks by himself. He wants a dog, begs his father to let him keep a stray that follows him home one day after school; but Pete says that they can't afford an animal.

"Who will take care of it? You?"

Jim nods, but his father disagrees. Jim gives up his hope of owning the stray pup when Pete scolds him for feeding the mutt. Jim winces and cries when his father kicks the dog in the ribs. The animal whimpers, quickly cowers, then limps away. Jim doesn't see the dog again.

As a second, third, and fourth grader, Jim endures bullying from other boys but most especially from Harry Link, a burly fellow who is almost twice his size and moves against him with determination. Harry tapes a thumbtack in Jim's chair at school in second grade. Jim sits, yelps in pain, reddens with embarrassment as other students giggle or guffaw; then he stands, removes the tack, sits back down at his desk and remains quiet. Jim never sits in a chair again without examining it first. Later that year, Harry stabs Jim's right thigh with a pencil as he strolls by him in class. Jim bites his tongue to tolerate the pain. When he bathes that night, he checks his leg to find a small piece of lead embedded in his flesh.

Harry gives Jim a black eye in third grade, pushing him down a short flight of steps, yelling at him to "get outta the way!" Jim gets up, gathers his books and strewn papers, goes on to his next class, comes in a bit late. The teacher scolds him, but Jim escapes a trip to the principal's office by apologizing. Harry is less aggressive in fourth grade, and by fifth grade he's bored with Jim; now he picks on several younger boys.

In sixth grade after a growth spurt over the previous summer, the tall 11 year old joins cross country track to race as a member of a school team. Jim is not only tall but skinny; and running makes him skinnier. Occasionally he crosses the finish line close to the front of the pack, but doesn't win. His team doesn't win either, for that matter. Pete doesn't attend any of his son's track meets. Jim is disappointed, and runs with a gloom surrounding him. His teammates soon avoid racing near him, making Jim a solitary figure on the cross country course.

While running one grey overcast morning when he's 13, Jim realizes he has no friends, no mother, no sisters or brothers, and not much of a father.

23 - MONEY JAR

Susan works hard at The Chart restaurant, makes good tips and begins to hide a small portion of these from Michael. She figures a day is coming when she needs to leave him, a day when his anger overwhelms her and truly endangers their child. Michael drinks like a fish, as far as Susan can tell. He spends his money on liquor whereas she spends hers on food for the three of them. She isn't able to pay the rent and utilities on her own, so every month she goes to Michael for help with these expenses. Michael reluctantly hands over cash to Susan, complaining that she doesn't know how to handle money. Susan nods, agrees.

The monies in Susan's hidden tip jar slowly increase, but she doesn't have enough to escape Michael. She can go to her parents, but she doesn't want to do this. Instead, each week she increases the amount she hides from Michael. If he discovers her deception, she knows she's in serious trouble.

At Christmas, the Holmes give Susan several hundred dollars without Michael's knowledge. Mr. Holmes insists that Susan spend this money on herself or on Judith. Her father says, "Don't waste it on that son of a bitch."

"Oh Dad; don't talk like that."

But, she takes the money and puts it in the jar. *That money is going to help so much when the time comes.*

And that time comes sooner than she anticipates. Judith is 7 years old when it happens. Michael arrives home after work, eats dinner, and leaves immediately. When he returns, it's late. He's drunk and already angry. He comes into the den where Susan knits a sweater while she listens to the radio. Coming up to her from behind, he grabs her hair as he has done before.

"You lazy bitch," he spits.

Stunned by his grip and his words, Susan tries to pull away. But Michael holds her hair tightly. He shakes her head back and forth and then slings her loose. Susan does not hesitate. She leaps up, runs into Judith's bedroom and locks the door. Hurriedly, she wraps Judith in her blanket and pulls her out of bed. "Hush," she says to her daughter. She reaches under the bed, into the corner of the rail, and into the box springs. She pulls out the lidded money jar, tucks it inside the blanket next to Judith. "We've gotta go, darling."

"Mommy?"

"Come on," says Susan, putting Judith down. "This way." She leads Judith with blanket and jar in tow to the connecting bathroom between her room and the master bedroom. The master bedroom door is locked from the inside of the bathroom. When Michael goes out to drink, Susan deliberately keeps this door locked for such an occasion as this.

She goes to the window, unlocks it, raises it and lifts Judith onto the top of the toilet. "Climb out, baby."

"I don't want to," says Judith.

"Just do it, sweetie. There's a box on the ground. Just lower yourself down. It'll be fine."

Judith obeys. When she is on the ground below the bathroom window, she looks up. Her mother awkwardly climbs through the window and joins her.

"Let's go," her mother whispers.

Woods line the edge of the back yard, and Susan leads her daughter into these. They make their way in the dark to the other side of the narrow line of forest into the parking lot behind a pharmacy. Susan looks at the sky; the stars are dim but clearly visible. *No rain. Thanks be to God.* She takes Judith by the wrist, "Where's the jar?"

Judith holds up the small glass jar. "Here it is, Mommy."

Susan sighs. "Good. Keep it safe."

"Yes, Mommy. I will."

Susan finds the pay phone outside the front of the J&K Pharmacy. She takes a nickel from the jar, puts it in the slot, waits for the dial tone. She carefully dials her parents' number. The phone rings twice. Alena answers, "Hello, this is the Holmes' residence. Alena speaking."

"Hello Mom. Can Dad pick us up?"

Alena asks tentatively, "What's happened?"

"Michael's drunk."

"And violent," says her mother.

"Yes."

"I'll be there in ten minutes."

"We're not at the house. Come to the J&K Pharmacy on Bobwhite."

"I'm leaving now."

Susan thanks her mother, hangs up the phone, takes Judith into the pharmacy to wait. She watches out the store's front window for any sign of Michael. She's not sure what to do if he shows up outside the J&K. Perhaps duck behind the cash register, perhaps hide between aisles. She doesn't know. She keeps watch.

Alena drives up in the Ford station wagon, honks the horn. Susan and Judith quickly walk out to the car. Susan puts Judith into the back seat, then sits beside her mother in front. She begins to cry.

Alena says, "Not in front of little ears, big eyes."

"Oh," says Susan. "Of course not." She stifles her tears, and relaxes into the seat.

Alena says to Judith, "I've got your doll house set up in your room at my house, sweetie pie."

Judith is stretched out on the back seat asleep.

The Holmes welcome their daughter and granddaughter into their house. They put Judith in her own room on the second floor near the main bathroom. Susan sleeps in the den on the sofa sleeper, pulling it out every night, putting it back every morning.

"Like camping," says Judith to her mother.

"Yes, honey; just like camping."

The next morning after her flight from Michael, he shows up at the Holmes' front door. He bangs on the door rather than ring the doorbell. Instead of opening the door, Joel Holmes speaks through it: "Go away, Michael."

"I want to see my wife and kid."

"Well," says Mr. Holmes, "you can't."

"You can't keep them from me."

"Michael, I'm not. They don't want to see you."

"Not Judith," screams Michael through the closed, locked door.

"Go away, Michael." Mr. Holmes doesn't wait. He turns from the door and heads back to the kitchen where Susan, Judith, and Alena wait. Susan sips her coffee while Judith drinks a glass of orange juice. Mrs. Holmes sings under her breath.

From the front of the house, they hear Michael bang repeatedly on the door; then, silence. A few minutes later, Alena notices Michael as he struts by the kitchen window.

"He's headed to the back door. Is it locked?"

"Yes," says Joel. "We've nothing to worry about." *Unless he breaks a window.* With that thought, Mr. Holmes picks up the receiver of the phone and dials 'zero'.

A woman answers, "Operator."

"I'd like the police please."

"One moment, sir. I'll connect you."

The sheriff's department answers the telephone. Mr. Holmes reports Michael Lesser as an intruder.

"An officer will be there momentarily. We've a car in your vicinity."

"Thank you," says Mr. Holmes.

At this point, Michael bangs on the back door. He peers in at them, raises his fist at Susan, glares at her parents. Mrs. Holmes rises, takes Judith's hand, leads her out of Michael's line of sight.

"Come on, sweetie pie. Let's take a bath." Judith only protests for a moment, then goes upstairs with her Granny.

Michael continues to bang against the door. Mr. Holmes walks to him, shouts through the glass, "The police are on the way, Michael. I suggest you leave while you can."

Michael laughs, but a siren is heard from the street at the front of the house. He startles, turns to run into the neighbor's yard and out of sight.

Joel invites the police officer into the living room. He introduces himself, "I'm Officer Wilson." When he sees Susan, he adds, "That's Officer Randy Wilson." Susan smiles at him. He blushes slightly, but she doesn't notice.

The young handsome officer sits on the couch where Susan sleeps and takes information from her. She speaks softly, so that Randy asks her to repeat herself several times. Finally, he rises. He says, "I'm probably not going to be able to charge him with anything but I'll pick him up for questioning. Maybe that'll scare him away for a while. You're going to need to file a complaint against him in front of a judge; get a restraining order so he can't come around you legally. As for keeping him away from his daughter, that's going to take some high fangled legal work." He smiles at Susan, shrugs his shoulders. "That's the best I can do right now - bringing him in, I mean."

"Thank you," says Susan.

"Meanwhile," says Officer Wilson, "you be careful."

She looks at him. "I will."

Randy touches Susan's right arm above the elbow and squeezes ever so slightly. His blue eyes twinkle at her. She smiles again. *Such a kind and good-looking man.*

24 - GI-JOE

Rick continues to eat but remains unable to keep food on his stomach. His weight drops precipitously. He drinks all the water he gets, and begs for more. Sometimes, the woman on the other side of the locked door responds by giving him another small cup of water. He thanks her through the slot every time. She says, "No problem-o, GI-Joe."

Every few days, two soldiers enter his cell and drag him out to another room. Before they do, one of them blindfolds him. His right shoulder above the heavy, loose cast is immovable, so Rick tries to carry his entire arm with his other. Often the soldiers strike his left arm to prevent him from carrying his injured wing. As gravity pulls his right arm toward the ground, Rick grimaces with pain, but he holds his tongue, refuses to cry out. He struggles to stay conscious. He knows if he faints, the men will drag him by that right arm and it will hurt even more when he regains consciousness.

The men take him to the cinderblock room with the drain in the floor; one of them removes his boots, the other ties him to the wooden chair. Then both leave. Screams that sound as if they come from Zach or Bob or Paul are piped into the room via an overhead speaker. The voices are extremely loud. Then, a soft female voice comes over the loudspeaker; this woman asks him questions that he completely ignores. He is unable to ignore them when he first is tied to this chair, but now he blocks the voice from his mind by thinking about Charlie and Annie and his mother especially. If he thinks about his father, he can only imagine his father striking Charlie, knocking his little brother to the sidewalk below the front porch steps, making Charlie's nose bleed profusely.

Today, a far door opens and a man Rick's not met enters the room. In his right hand is a small black object with a metal end and a wire hanging from the other end. Rick's body breaks out in a fine sweat again. *Oh god, what's that?*

The man walks over, plugs the wired end of the object into a socket in the ceiling above the chair where Rick is tied. The metal end slowly begins to smoke; the hot metallic smell rises from it and enters Rick's nose. Soon, the metal glows red. *Name. Rank. Serial Number.*

The man takes the object, walks slowly up to Rick, strips what's left of Rick's shirt from his chest and places the hot end of the metal on Rick's skin. The smell of his flesh burning comes at him at the exact moment the searing pain reaches his brain. He screams despite his best effort to resist. As Rick drifts into unconsciousness, the man splashes icy water in his face.

"No, no. No sleep for you," says the man.

Rick looks at the man wild-eyed. "What do you want?" he asks.

"Why did you and your men try to bomb Hanoi?"

Rick struggles to remember what he's supposed to say. *What is it? It's simple. I know... oh, name, rank, serial number.* He tells the man his name, his rank, and tries to recite his serial number. At the moment, the number doesn't come to mind. He shakes his head, laughs nervously. "I can't remember what you want to know. I'm sorry." He forgets that his serial number is clearly printed on the dog tags that hang from his neck.

"Did you mean to fire bomb babies?"

"Babies?" asks Rick. He's confused.

"Yes, you burn babies."

Rick struggles not to protest. He repeats his name, his rank, again forgetting his serial number. He apologizes again for his ignorance.

The man strikes Rick's left cheek, then comes again with the hot metal. When the metal touches Rick's right upper chest, he screams again, faints. Icy water dumped over his head brings him back. The man is close in Rick's face, whispering, "You are alone. No one is here to help you. Only I can help you. Why do you and your crew bomb Hanoi? Why do you burn babies?"

Rick shakes his head. He gives his name, rank, and tries again to state his serial number. It's correct, but Rick is uncertain. Only later does he realize he knows it so well he can't get it wrong even under duress.

The man unplugs the black object, walks out of the room. Five minutes later, the two soldiers enter, untie Rick, blindfold him again and return him to his cell. He's tossed onto the floor in the far corner. He gladly releases his hold on consciousness; faints.

A rapid tap from the wall wakes Rick who rolls over to rise up on his left arm. He leans against the wall, and taps back to Zach, "Yes?"

"You okay?"

"I've been better, but yes."

"Get ready," warns Zach.

"What now?" asks Rick.

Zach taps, "They broke Paul's legs."

"What?"

Zach taps out the details. Apparently, the men drag Paul from his cell out into a small outdoor enclosure and smash his legs with the same heavy mallet used on Zach's big toe.

"Oh God," taps Rick. "I'm not sure I can't take this any more."

"You and me both." Zach is quiet for a few moments, then taps, "That's one heavy mallet, Rick. My big toe is still mangled up. I totally lost the nail."

"Is Paul okay?"

"He's in a lot of pain; of course he can't walk. But he's hanging tough."

"Tell him -" Rick stops. He doesn't know what Zach should tell Paul. What can you tell someone who is in this situation?

Zach taps, "Wait."

Rick stops breathing. He waits. He hears Zach cry out, presumably for his benefit. He hears Zach yell, "Oh god, this is it. Bye boys!" After this, nothing comes through the wall. Rick closes his eyes, listens even though he doesn't want to hear. The screams come soon after, blood-curdling and guttural as during previous torture episodes.

Rick sweats; his sweat is cold, and beads up all over him. He waits. He knows the lock is going to click, and the men are going to come for him next.

When Zach returns to his cell, he taps out, "Still alive, brother." Rick smiles, relaxes, sleeps with his back to the wall. Sometime in the middle of the night, the lock clicks, waking Rick. The two men enter, drag him out into the small outdoor enclosure and smash his right knee with a huge heavy mallet. He screams louder than he thinks possible.

25 - JOINT CUSTODY

During their divorce, Michael Lesser fights Susan for joint custody of Judith, and wins. The judge is an elderly man, and although he recognizes Susan's concerns, he also acknowledges that a father has rights to his child as much as a mother.

Judith spends summers and every other major holiday with her father. Michael moves from West Virginia to North Carolina where he works in a tire factory. Judith rides a bus from Beckley to Fayetteville in late May right after school ends, and returns a few days before school starts. Summers are hot in Fayetteville as contrasted with Beckley which sits in the mountains. Judith learns to swim, spends most days at the local public swimming pool. She also plays badminton with some girls in her father's neighborhood. He buys her a bicycle which she uses to get around while he is at work. The amount of freedom she enjoys is considerable when compared to the lack of freedom with her mother and her grandparents, who keep a tight rein on her when she is in Beckley.

Judith is wary, however, when she is with her father. Michael remains highly unpredictable. He may come home drunk and angry, drunk and cheery, drunk and sleepy, drunk and hungry. Occasionally, he comes home sober. Even sober, he is mean at times.

Judith functions as cook and housekeeper for her father when he is home. She makes his dinner, cleans his dishes, and washes his clothes. She keeps the house in order. When he is at work, Judith has full run of the house and is able to go anywhere in Fayetteville her bicycle will take her. And, she takes advantage of her freedom. She bikes all around Fayetteville, finds a wonderful bakery where she buys bread for their meals, several farmers' markets where she buys fresh fruits and vegetables, and a butcher where she buys great cuts of meat, usually beef. Michael puts two baskets on the back wheel of the bike so that Judith is able to haul her goodies home. He also doesn't hesitate to give her money for these purchases; for some reason, he trusts her in ways in which he can not trust his ex-wife, Susan.

Judith *is* trustworthy. She does not spend her father's money on herself unless he tells her she can - which is a rare occurrence. Instead, she brings home his change and places it in the center of the kitchen table; next to the change she puts the receipts. When he comes in, his first stop is the table. He picks up the change, but leaves the receipts for later.

"What's for dinner, baby girl?"

"Ribeye steaks, Dad," she says, "and mashed potatoes with gravy. And, we've got a tossed salad to round it out. What do you want to drink?" Michael opens the refrigerator, pulls out a beer. He lifts it in a form of a salute. She looks away, nods her head. The table is set. "Sit down, Dad. I'll get a glass of milk, and join you."

Michael sits at the head of the table; Judith joins him, sitting on his left. She hands the salt and pepper shakers to her father, then bows her head slightly, closes her eyes, whispers a quick prayer, raises her head and begins to serve him first. He stares at her while she places a large steak on his plate, then a heap of mashed potatoes and a full ladle of gravy. She pushes the salad bowl toward him. "Do you want French dressing, Dad?"

"Sure," he says.

Judith pours a tablespoon of the dressing on his salad. He takes the salad dressing bottle from her and pours a generous amount on his salad.

"That's better," he barks.

"Yes, Dad."

He swigs his beer, and cuts a bite of the ribeye. He puts a large piece in his mouth, speaks around it, "That's good, darling."

"Thanks, Dad."

He takes a large bite of the mashed potatoes. "Not enough salt, Judith. How many times?"

"Sorry Dad. There's the salt, right there."

He grabs the salt shaker, shakes a considerable amount of salt onto the gravy that Judith ladles onto the mound of potatoes on her father's plate. He takes another bite. "Ah, much better. I wish you'd learn."

"Sorry Dad."

Michael shakes his head, makes noises which indicate he enjoys his food despite his complaints. Judith understands the contrast; she lives with him over several summers. When he finishes his meal, Michael takes another beer from the refrigerator, goes into the den and turns on the radio. He sits on the couch while Judith scrapes the plates and washes the dishes in the double sink. When she finishes, she comes into the den, leans over, kisses her father on the cheek.

"Good night, Dad."

"Goodnight, Judith." He pats her at her waistline.

With that, Judith goes to her room on the back end of the small house, closes and quietly locks her door, crawls into bed fully clothed, and goes to sleep. She's almost 11, and afraid of the man in the den.

Stretched out on the couch with the radio on in the background, her father continues to drink beer after beer after beer until he passes out. Outside, the sun is setting in the North Carolina sky.

26 - OPEN LOCK

Judith stands in front of her locker. She wears a dark brown turtleneck sweater with a plaid skirt that comes just above her knees with matching brown knee high stockings on her legs. On her feet are a pair of brown and white lace-up Oxfords. Her hair is long and silky black; her skin pale, her eyes dark brown. Jim is shy, but he's struck by the beauty of this girl.

Judith spins the combination lock once again, and tries to open it but the lock won't release. She looks at Jim who first looks away, then back into her eyes. He smiles, shrugs his shoulders. He ventures, "I'm not sure I can make it work any better." He comes close to the locker to help; is shocked that this girl doesn't back up. He looks at her again. "May I?"

"Oh, sure."

Jim takes the combination lock in his hands, looks at the girl again.

"The combination?"

Judith hands this tall, skinny boy with tight curly hair and fuzz all over his face a slender piece of paper with the number printed on it.

Jim plays with the lock, and after the second attempt, says, "I think it's broken."

"Well, I thought so," says Judith.

Jim's hands sweat. He glances at the beautiful girl who smiles at him. He relaxes and smiles back. Jim leads Judith to the main office of the school so she can request maintenance for her locker. She thanks him.

She's new in town, and Jim decides to ask her if she might like to get a coke. He's never asked anyone to go or do anything with him before. His mouth is dry, but he manages to say the words, "Wanna get a coke?"

Judith surprises him by saying she'd love to get a coke with him. After school, Jim takes her across the street to the Sweet Shop, buys each of them a coke and suggests they share a chocolate cupcake. Judith grins, says, "Sure."

A few weeks later, Jim asks Judith to the Junior prom. She accepts. She wears a lovely white dress with white shoes. Jim wears a vest, white shirt, tie and black slacks he borrows from his father's closet with nice dark shoes of his own.

"Jim and Judith make a handsome couple," says one of Judith's teachers.

Jim's teachers whisper at the refreshment table. "Can you believe it?" says one. Another teacher who particularly dislikes his student says, "And to think such a pretty girl-"

Jim dances better than either he or Judith expect. Jim smiles, beaming for the first time he remembers. At the end of the evening, he ventures to give his date a light kiss on the cheek. Judith turns her face so that Jim's lips meet hers. He lingers. His first kiss is with the girl he marries right after high school graduation.

Despite having no friends, Jim manages to find a girlfriend, gain a wife, and keep both. His father, Pete doesn't notice until Jim moves out.

27 - ORDINARY BEERS

Dave Pissleton hands Charlie a hot dog and a beer. "Here you go, Chuck."

"Thanks Dave."

Charlie sits on the railroad track, tucks his heels up under the edge of the metal rail, and takes a huge bite from one end of the hot dog. He mumbles, "Gosh, that's good."

"You think *that's* good! Try the beer."

Charlie takes the cap off the beer bottle with the bottle opener hanging from his belt loop. He takes a large swallow; the taste is bitter and heavy. He's not sure he likes this one.

Dave says, "That's a German beer. Came all the way from Germany. My dad brought it back with him."

Charlie looks at Dave. *So what?* Instead, he says, "Hey man, that's cool."

"Yeah, my dad travels all over the world. I've had so many different types of beer from just everywhere." He holds up the German ale.

"You like it?"

Charlie considers. He says, "It's okay."

"Okay! That's the last time I waste good beer on you, Chuckie."

Charlie drinks cheap beer; it's the only kind he can afford. *Good German beer is wasted on me.* He doesn't care what beer tastes like; he cares what it does for him. He glances at Dave. *Now this guy is a waste of my time.* Charlie decides, then and there, to slowly break it off with Dave Pissleton. As soon as he decides this, he grows reluctant. Dave is a great source of free alcohol. He weighs the consequences of ending his friendship with his neighbor. *Maybe next year.*

"Yeah," says Charlie, "you should save that good stuff for someone else. I've not a developed palate, you know."

Dave laughs. "For sure," he says. He finishes off his beer, takes Charlie's and finishes it off too. "Come on. I'll pick you out something cheap." He balances on the rail, walks quickly toward their houses. Charlie follows behind, balancing on the rail considerably better than Dave. Twenty minutes later, they are in Dave's back yard.

Dave opens the garage which - typical of this neighborhood - is separate from his house. He grabs Charlie's wrist, pulls him into the dark storage area, then closes the garage door quickly and quietly. "Here," he says. He pulls Charlie along. In the corner is a large refrigerator plugged into the wall. Charlie hears its hum. When Dave opens the refrigerator door, Charlie sees row upon row of beer bottles on their sides, caps toward him. Charlie realizes hundreds of different kinds of beer are stored here. *A motherlode!* He looks at Dave Pissleton. *Maybe you aren't a waste of my time.*

"Happy, Chuckie?"

Charlie ignores that Dave calls him by a name he abhors. He says, "Oh yeah, very."

Dave whispers, "Only thing, you can't tell anybody about this. You can't tell anyone I showed you where my dad keeps his beer."

"This is your dad's?"

"Well sure, dope."

Charlie's morale drops. *How can I get away with drinking this stuff?*

"Don't worry," says Dave. "It's not like we could drink it all!"

Charlie looks at the beers stacked on each shelf of the huge refrigerator. "Maybe not," he says.

"Oh gosh, Chuckie." And with that, Dave starts to close the door.

"Hey," protests Charlie. "Aren't you gonna share with me?"

"Oh yeah," says Dave. He reaches into the cold and pulls out one from inside the door. He hands it to Charlie, who uses his bottle opener. He takes a long drink. The beer is ordinary. Charlie smiles. He nods his head approvingly, and points to another bottle in the refrigerator door while he chugs the one in his other hand.

28 - ANNIE GRADUATES

When Annie graduates from Springboro High School, she doesn't know Charlie's location. The last time she sees him, he's playing as first-string catcher for the Toledo Mud Hens. At the end of his fourth season in the minor leagues, Charlie is abruptly fired. Annie doesn't fully understand the reason for Charlie being let go. She knows he's a great catcher, so she's understandably confused. She's never heard anything negative about her brother from anyone except from their father, who doesn't seem to like Charles very much. This too confuses Annabelle, who loves and likes Charlie very much.

Judith says Charles is likely somewhere in the south. She tells Annie she knows that after being fired Charles is in Atlanta for a few months; but from there, she's not certain. Judith keeps all emotion from her voice when she speaks to Annabelle, averting her eyes when her daughter appears bewildered. Annie can not believe she is going to graduate from high school without Charlie there to cheer for her.

Instead of Charlie sitting in the high school auditorium, her older brother Rick is seated in the third row. Richard comes back from the Vietnam war alive, much to the surprise and delight of family and community. Rick is now 27. His right arm is shorter than his left by approximately a quarter inch, and stiff from a damaged shoulder. He has several visible scars across his left cheekbone, and other hidden scars across his back and chest. Three on his chest are deep burn marks with another scar appearing in the shape of a star from a bayonet thrust. Under his pants, Rick also has brutal appearing scars to both knees and thighs. Rick sits quietly, excited to see his little sister, Annabelle receive her diploma. He is in full dress uniform, and still as handsome as ever.

A year earlier, Judith is overwhelmed when she and Jim receive an official letter informing them that Rick, their older son is a prisoner of war in northern Vietnam. During his debriefing Zachary Hunter, a crew gunner and fellow prisoner of war released a year before Richard, reports the pilot's survival, location, and general condition. Judith is shocked that her son Richard is not dead, but alive in a dank prison in northern Vietnam, behind enemy lines. The letter arrives several months after Charlie, her younger son disappears from Ohio, and then from Atlanta. Despite multiple phone calls to police stations in and around Atlanta, Judith and Jim are unable to determine the whereabouts of their younger son. Judith wants so much to tell Charlie that Rick is alive. She also desires to know Charlie is okay.

"Annabelle Louise Logan," announces the principal of Springboro High School. Annie walks across the stage in her black cap and gown with golden trim, takes Mr. Morrison's offered hand with her right hand while grasping her diploma with her left. She smiles in the direction of the camera, and walks off stage.

Later, she asks Rick, "Did Mom tell you I'm going to Columbia?"

"No! Wow!" he says. "I'm impressed."

Annie realizes she's not told Rick about her dream to study medicine. She smiles, says, "Rick, I'm going pre-med."

"Pre-med?"

"Yes, I'm gonna be a doctor."

Rick laughs, "That's great, Annabelle."

Annie looks at her feet. She's suddenly uncomfortable. *Not like talking to Charlie. Charlie? Where are you?* She glances at Rick's right arm, then looks away. She says, "I've got something for you, Rick."

"You do," he says. "On your graduation day, you've a gift for me?"

Annie blushes slightly, nods. "Well, I meant to give it to you when you first got home, but -" She reaches under the sleeve of her black gown and removes something. She hands it to Rick who sees Annie has given him a KIA copper bracelet with his full name etched across its surface. Tears form and stay in his eyes. He looks up at his baby sister. She says, "Charlie's got one, too. Wherever he is."

"Thank you, Annabelle," says Rick. He doesn't stand up, but puts his left arm up to touch and then squeeze Annie's upper arm.

Annie nods her head again, then waits a moment, shifts her weight twice. She says, "Well, I'm going over there to talk to Mary and Betty Sue. You remember them?"

Rick turns to look at the two girls in black cap and gown with golden trim, and shakes his head. "No, I don't Annabelle." The two girls obviously remember Rick. Both giggle and wave.

Annie blushes, hesitates; then says, "Well, that's okay. I'll see you later."

"See you later," repeats Rick. He sits in the same chair he sits in for the graduation ceremony. The seats around him are empty. Only a few people mill about the auditorium at the high school. He puts the copper KIA bracelet in his suit pocket, struggles to stand, begins to slowly inch his way out of the row, grasping each chair back as he moves.

29 - JIM'S SEARCH

In early September, after Annabelle leaves for Columbia in New York City, Jim takes the old Chevy truck, gases it up, and drives south toward Atlanta. He's determined to find his younger son. He insists that Judith and Rick not come along. Jim finds it particularly challenging to keep Rick from going with him. *Maybe Rick feels obligated to protect Charles from me.* He decides to leave in the wee hours of the morning before either Judith or Rick wake.

The drive is easy except for over the Appalachian Mountains before he reaches Chattanooga, Tennessee. The truck nearly overheats going up the long, steep grades and the brakes feel as if they're failing as the truck goes down the longer, steeper grades on the other side of the mountain ridge. But the Chevy doesn't fail Jim; it goes over the mountain range and eventually reaches Chattanooga where Jim finds a cheap motel off the highway. The next morning, he and the Chevy are on the road again.

When Jim drives into Atlanta, his first stop is the bus station downtown. He speaks with several people in the ticket booths, shows old photographs of a younger Charlie as well as a few, more recent publicity shots of Charlie as first string catcher for the Toledo Mud Hens. No one recognizes the young man in the pictures. Jim spends the night in another even cheaper motel. When he sleeps, he dreams of his younger son. He dreams his fist contacts Charlie's chin over and over and over again. He sees his booted foot strike the back of

Charlie's head, and sees Charlie tumble down the concrete steps to land on the sidewalk. Charlie's head splits open like a watermelon, its red guts and black seeds spilling out everywhere. Jim wakes in a heavy sweat.

In the morning, Jim stops by the main police station in the downtown area, shows the photographs again to the dispatcher, to several officers walking by in the hallway. One officer stops, stares at the picture of Charlie Logan as catcher. He smiles, "I think I saw this guy play."

"When?" asks Jim, momentarily excited.

"Oh," says the middle aged man, "It's been a few years. I think I saw him play in Spartanburg against the Phillies. But he couldn't have been there. That's a Toledo uniform." He points to the photograph. "The Mud Hens don't play the Phillies."

Jim offers, "Charlie used to play for the Statesville Tigers."

"Yeah, that's it. He was a Tiger. I remember him. He's damn good."

Jim tears up, surprised at the level of his feeling for Charles. He tells the officer, "Yes, he is."

"Come on, man," says the policeman. "Sit over here. What's wrong?"

"I can't find him," says Jim.

"What do you mean, you can't find him?"

Jim tells the officer that Charlie lost his position as catcher with the Mud Hens last year. "I don't even know why really. It's all a bit vague."

"Oh, I'm sorry to hear that."

"Yeah, he sort of disappeared."

"Disappeared?"

"Yes, just vanished. The last time we heard from him, he was here in Atlanta. He called us from the bus station. That's where I was last night, showing his picture. No one could tell me anything. I don't know where he is."

"Did you file a missing person report?"

Jim looks bewildered. "How do I do that?"

"Come on. I'll help you," says the policeman. He turns, extends his hand. "By the way, I'm Tom McNamara."

"Jim Logan."

"Nice to meet you, Mr. Logan." Tom takes Jim into a small room after gathering several forms from the dispatcher's desk. He seats the distraught man at a large table, gives him a pen, and instructs him to fill in all the spaces on the forms. "When you're finished, let me know. I'll turn them in for you. Okay?"

"Right; thanks."

"I'll be out there in the hall. I'll wait."

"Thank you Mr. McNamara."

"Tom."

"I'm Jim." He sits at the table awkwardly with the pen and papers in his hand.

Tom smiles, walks from the room, waits in the hallway beside the dispatcher's desk. He tells the dispatcher how sorry he feels for Mr.

Logan. The dispatcher looks up from her work, nods, goes back to her paperwork.

In the small room, Jim quietly fills out the forms. His hands shake as he writes his son's full name in the space labeled 'Missing Person.'

30 - LOPSIDED MAN

When Rick awakens in his cell the next morning, his right knee is black, blue and swollen. He is unable to bend it or stretch it out. He rolls over onto his left side, pushes up with his only good arm and pulls himself backwards to lean against the wall. He examines his knees. The left one is fine, but the right knee looks like the pulp of a red plum. Rick winces, thinking of the mallet as it strikes.

He sighs. He taps on the wall, listens.

Zach taps, "Hey."

"Hey. Well, we're alive."

"Yes, we are."

"Do you have knees?" taps Rick.

"I've got one."

"Me, too."

"Which one did the gooks leave you?" asks Zach.

"My left, oddly enough."

"I guess they didn't want to completely cripple you."

"I guess not," says Rick. *I'm a lopsided man.* He takes the right sleeve of his ragged shirt in his left hand and tears the whole sleeve away from the shoulder seam. He wraps the cloth around his damaged knee and ties a small knot in the back.

"Can you walk, Zach?"

"Not hardly," taps Zach. "You?"

"No way." *I can't even crawl.*

The morning ticks away; the sun is high when Rick realizes he's been asleep with his back against the wall. When he stirs, his right knee spits pain - sharp at first then a dull throb that goes on and on. Tears are in his eyes. He takes a deep breath and tries to relax the muscles in his right thigh. He begins to take the Chevy truck apart, and put it back together in his mind. But the pain is distracting. He can't focus. *Maybe I should take a trip to the moon and back.* He remembers the hot summer evening in 1969 as he sits with his parents, Annabelle and Charlie watching the black and white fuzzy television picture as Neil Armstrong takes a small step for one man and a great leap for mankind. He imagines himself in the Apollo 11 capsule as he watches the surface of the moon rush up toward him and his companion, Buzz Aldrin. *What happened to Neil? Ah well, no matter. I'm here.* He opens the capsule, steps out onto the steps, slowly moves down to touch the grey dust of the lunar surface. *Some pain in my right leg. Oh, no matter. Keep going.* Rick leaps from the last step, speaks Armstrong's immortal words, then bounces across the landscape. He breathes in an interesting mix of oxygen and other gases about which he knows little to nothing. He's heady, thrilled to experience the limited gravity of the moon. *No need to crawl here. I'm bouncing!*

Zach's tapping interrupts Rick's imaginary journey. The tapping seems frantic. *A warning. Maybe I'm losing oxygen from my suit. I'm suffocating.* Then Rick remembers. *I'm a prisoner of war in Vietnam.* He taps, "What?"

"They're coming!"

The lock across the cell clicks, the door opens. Four men enter. Rick shakes his head at the men, then yells, "No, no, no. Leave me alone!" Rick yells so that Zach is able to hear him through the thin wall between their cells.

The four men pick Rick up by all four extremities. Each man grabs an arm, a leg and together they carry Rick out as if he is a large sack of potatoes. Rick screams as the men on the right lead and the men on his left follow. He faints despite the men screaming at him, presumably in an attempt to keep him awake and in pain.

31 - DAY DREAMS

Her first night in New York City at Columbia University, Annie stretches out on the bottom bunk in her dormitory room, falls asleep and dreams Charlie is in a hole. Apparently, he's fallen into this dark, deep hole and can't climb out. Annie looks down into the darkness and softly calls out for Charlie. "Are you okay?" No response. Annie reaches down into the darkness to touch her brother if possible. She can't reach him. She sits on the edge of the hole with her calves and feet swinging in the dark. *So dark, I can't see my own feet.* She waits. *Surely Charlie will climb out. Surely he will.*

Suddenly a baseball as big as the moon sails up from the hole and strikes Annie directly in the center of her forehead. She falls backwards, lands on her upper back and shoulders. Her head snaps back, hits the ground. A welt begins to form in the center of her forehead. She laughs, then feels blood flow from both ears. *Oh my. Wake up now. Wake up.*

Annie wakes with a start. The room is lit from the window and a street lamp outside. Her roommate, Linda is asleep in the upper bunk. Annie is able to hear her breathing, steady and quiet. Annie feels her ears and her forehead. *No blood. No welt. Charlie? You're okay Charlie. You aren't going to lose it. I promise.*

Annie goes back to sleep and wakes with a slight headache the next morning. She rises, readies herself, and goes to breakfast in the college cafeteria with Linda. Linda is from Madison, a city in southern Indiana, its downtown right up against the banks of the Ohio River. She's at Columbia to study fine arts, particularly painting. Linda tells Annie the first morning how much she loves to paint; one of her favorite subjects is cows. She enjoys painting black and white heifers standing in fields of green grass and golden hay bales; the sky smooth and bright baby blue.

"Funny, huh?" she asks Annie.

"Not really."

"What are you majoring in?" asks Linda.

"Pre-med," says Annie.

"Oh, you're going to be a doctor."

"Yes, I want to be a pediatrician."

"Cool, man."

"And you're gonna be a great artist."

Linda blushes, "Maybe."

After a quick breakfast, Linda and Annie part ways. Annie goes to her classes; Linda goes to hers. Annie takes sixteen credit hours this first semester, four classes are for three credits each, two classes are for two credits each: Introduction to English, Biology, Introduction to Psychology, Introduction to Sociology are the three credit hour classes; Biology lab and Fencing are the two credit hour classes. *I'm going to have a busy busy semester.*

Her first day consists of meeting her professors, some of her classmates, purchasing her books and other materials, and finding her way around the Columbia campus.

The first week, Annie has Charlie on her mind constantly, but as the coursework gets underway and the work becomes more and more challenging, Annie begins to find whole days during which Charlie is only a brief thought. As the semester progresses, she thinks about her brother less and less. Rick calls her long distance the third week-end she's in New York. He asks her how she's doing.

"I'm fine," she says, then silence.

"Dad hasn't found out anything more about Charles."

"Oh," she says. "That's too bad."

"Yes," says her brother on the other end of the line.

"Dad is still in Georgia?"

"Yes, he's been traveling around the Atlanta area looking for anything that might tell us where Charlie is."

"Oh," says Annie. Then, she adds, "I hope Charlie's okay."

Rick offers comfort, "I'm sure he is."

"Yes, he probably is."

"Okay," says Rick. "Well, I wanted to check in with you."

"Thanks Richard," says Annie.

"Okay," he says. "Okay, well, bye."

"Bye." Annie hesitates, then adds, "Kiss -" but the line goes dead as Rick hangs up.

32 - COLUMBIA DAYS

Jim drives south toward Macon the end of his third week in Georgia. He briefly stops at the airport just south of Atlanta, shows Charlie's picture to several airport workers and even to a few travelers. No one recognizes the young man in the photograph.

That same night in another cheap motel, Jim realizes it's time to go back to Ohio. *Judith and Rick need me. I can't help Charles any more. I can't find him. And I'm sick of being on the road, being with myself.*

The next morning, Jim takes the Chevy back through Atlanta toward Chattanooga, over the mountains and into Kentucky. By eleven o'clock that night, Jim crosses the Ohio River, enters Cincinnati where he stops for gasoline. An hour later, he pulls into his driveway in Turtle Creek Township. The house is completely dark. He fumbles with the lock, opens the front door and comes into the foyer. He locks the house, turns, startles to see Rick seated on the step at the base of the staircase.

"What the hell," gasps Jim.

"I was going to say the same thing, Dad. You're lucky I didn't kill you."

His father looks at him, then shrugs his shoulders. "Yeah, I guess so. Sorry I should have called."

"You don't think I can kill you."

Jim stares blankly in the dimness of the foyer. He looks at Rick's legs and his mismatched arms. Jim shrugs his shoulders again. "Oh, I don't know, Richard. I'm tired." He pushes passed his son who remains seated on the bottom step. "I'm going to bed."

"Goodnight, Dad."

Is that sarcasm? "Goodnight, Richard." He starts up the stairs.

Rick says, "Don't scare Mom."

Yes, he's taking verbal punches at me. Jim stops behind Rick, looks down on him. "What's with you, anyway?"

Rick turns, looks up at his father. "Oh, I don't know. You're gone more than three weeks, and you call us once. Poor Mom; she's been at her wit's end."

"So have I, Richard."

"Really?" says Rick. "Since when do you care about Charlie?"

Jim sighs. He tells Rick, "Goodnight, son."

"Okay," says Rick. "Goodnight."

Jim stops, turns, sits on the fourth step above Rick. He sighs again. "Son," he starts, "I'm sorry."

Rick looks closely at his father's face. In the semi-darkness, the man appears weary and perhaps sad.

"I'm sorry I hit Charles."

Rick struggles to rise, moves up to sit next to his father. He awkwardly places his own right arm around his father's upper back. Rick says, "Dad."

"I know I was too tough on him. I know it." Jim studies Richard's eyes. "I want you to know that I know. And that I'm sorry."

Rick continues to hold his father's shoulders even though his own right arm is stiff and hurts. "That's good of you, Dad. I mean, I'm glad you told me this."

"Yeah, it's been on my mind a lot since Charles disappeared in Atlanta."

"You didn't find any trace of him?"

"A cop recognized him; saw Charles play in Spartanburg when he was with the Tigers. But, that was a while ago now. So, no. I didn't find anything that would tell us where he went."

"I wonder why he hasn't contacted us."

Jim looks at Rick. "Charles thinks you're dead."

Rick drops his chin, looks at his feet. "Yes."

"Haunts me, Richard. It really haunts me."

"I know," says Rick. "Charlie haunts me, too."

Jim sighs once more, and adds, "Poor Annabelle."

Rick tears up, "Poor Charlie, Dad."

In New York, Annie wakes. She sits up, almost strikes her head on the metal rail of the bed above hers. She looks around the room. Annie hears Linda quietly snoring. She stares at the closet door, slightly ajar. *Nothing there.* She listens, hears a few people on the sidewalk below her dorm window. *Charlie? Charlie. Oh, okay. Yes, you're not going to lose it. Yes, I promise. Charlie?*

Charlie startles awake. He hears Annie's voice in his head. Now she asks him a question, wants to know where he is. He looks around. He's in a shelter, sleeping on a hard mattress as thin as several blankets wrapped together in a worn muslin sheet. Charlie and this makeshift mattress are stretched on an army cot in a large aluminum building in downtown Columbia, South Carolina. Charlie speaks softly, "I'm right here, Annie-belle. I'm okay."

Oh, okay.

"I'm not lost."

Yes, you're not going to lose it.

Charlie whispers, "You think so?"

Yes, I promise. Charlie?

A woman in an odd uniform walks by Charlie's cot with a small dim flashlight in her left hand. She keeps the light from striking sleeping people, but she still monitors the situation in the large shelter. Charlie shakes his head as if to tell Annie he can't speak any longer. He closes his eyes, falls into sleep.

Annie sits on the edge of her lower bunk bed, and waits in the silence. She doesn't hear Charlie again. Still she sits in the dark and listens. She listens to Linda breathing, now and then snoring.

In the morning, Annie walks to the cafeteria, eats a large breakfast of two sunny-side-up eggs, two pieces of buttered toast, a cup of coffee and a tall glass of orange juice. She takes a red apple with her to her first class that starts at 8 a.m. Through the day, Annie travels on foot from one class to another, has a big lunch, and a good dinner, studies through the evening and goes to sleep relatively early.

As for Charlie, he sleeps on the lumpy mattress and wakes stiff in the morning. His breakfast consists of dry toast, coffee and a small glass of cloudy apple juice. The rest of the day, he spends looking for work. Late in the morning, he finds day work digging ditches, picking up construction debris, and painting over graffiti on the side of a gas station. At the end of the day, he's paid thirty-three dollars in cash.

That night, he makes his way back to the shelter, has a simple meal of an over-ripe banana and watery milk over a cheap dry cereal that tastes of stale corn. Charlie sleeps on the same mattress, and wakes the next day to repeat this routine. Throughout the day, he doesn't think about his mother or father, or even about Rick. Although he doesn't know where she is, Charlie only thinks of and speaks to Annie-belle, his beautiful baby sister.

CARLEY EASON EVANS

33 - NEW MAN

The handsome police officer calls on Susan within the first month of the finalization of her divorce from Michael Lesser. She lives with her parents; it's mid-summer and Judith is with her father in Fayetteville, North Carolina. Susan calls Judith long-distance. In the kitchen, Michael answers the phone. "Hello," he says curtly.

"Hello Michael."

"Oh, it's you."

"Yes," says Susan. "May I speak with Judith please?"

Michael lies, "She's not here."

Judith comes into the kitchen, takes the receiver from her father's hand. "That's not true." She puts the phone to her ear, and says, "Hello, this is Judith."

"Hey honey!"

"Oh, hi Mom. What's going on?"

Susan tells her daughter that the divorce is final. Judith listens, nods, glances at her father who remains standing next to her. "Excuse me, Dad. Please."

Michael grunts, but leaves the kitchen. Judith hears the radio click on, and the sports' announcer screaming a score. She turns her attention to the phone, "Okay Mom. He's left."

Susan tells her daughter all about the divorce. "Yes, the judge has ordered you to spend your summers with your father just like it's set up now."

"But," says Judith, "that's so unfair. That judge didn't even ask me what I want."

Susan says, "Well, I guess we can appeal that. I think. I'll talk to my lawyer."

Judith asks, "Can you afford to do that, Mom?"

"Not really," admits her mother. "But your grandparents will help us. I know they will."

"Maybe I can't win, Mom."

Michael glides passed her, goes to the kitchen sink, runs tap water into a dirty glass. He rinses out his mouth, spits, opens the refrigerator, takes out a beer, opens it with a bottle opener that's attached to the side of the icebox. He glides passed Judith again, glares at her briefly. Then he's back on the couch in the den, listening to a ballgame of some kind.

Judith says, "I gotta go."

"Bye honey." The line goes dead as Susan adds, "I'm so sorry."

The next weekend, the Holmes' door bell rings. Joel answers the door. A familiar police officer stands on the front stoop, smiling. He has a hand behind his back.

"Yes?" says Joel. "May I help you, officer?"

"Is Susan home?"

"Yes, I think she is. Has she done something wrong, sir?"

"Oh, no. Nothing like that." And the young officer blushes. He shows Mr. Holmes the flowers he holds behind his back. "I've come to ask her to dinner and a movie."

"Oh, oh," says Joel. "Come on in. Have a seat. I'll go find her."

Susan is surprised but delighted to see the handsome and kind policeman she remembers from the day she first left Michael. The man is seated on the pull-out sofa where she sleeps every night. He has no idea. She comes into the parlor, sits beside him. "Hello, Randy."

"You remember my name," he says.

"Of course I do," she says. "You remember mine, too. Don't you?"

"Yes, Susan." He laughs. "I remember your name."

He laughs again. Then he sort of jumps, like he's excited. He says, "I almost forgot. These are for you." Randy gives Susan the bouquet of flowers. She smells them, smiles at him. "They're beautiful. Thank you."

Randy takes Susan to dinner at a fancy restaurant not unlike The Chart where Susan now works full-time as the head waitress. Susan is not used to being waited on; she sits in wonder at the service and the exquisite food in this restaurant. Then, they go to see the new movie *Heaven Can Wait* at the small theater near the restaurant. Susan cries several times during the film. Randy isn't too impressed with the story, but Susan loves it.

Randy dates Susan a year, then asks her to marry him one evening when the stars are fully out, and the moon is pale and low in the night sky. She says, "Yes."

Judith attends the wedding. She never sees her mother happier.

After the summer with her father, Judith naturally moves in with her mother and her mother's new husband. Randy treats Judith respectfully and with kindness. He doesn't pretend to be her father; rather, he supports Susan in her role as mother to a young girl becoming a young woman.

Judith's life stabilizes. She no longer lives in fear. Randy and Susan go back to the judge with a new lawyer, and change Michael's custody to liberal visitation rights. With increased restrictions and with the distance Michael must travel to see his daughter, Judith sees less and less of her biological father. At first, she's oddly and unexpectedly sad. Eventually she sees that as she moves into puberty, her father becomes more and more violent toward her. *Makes sense. I'm turning into my mother, and he hates her.*

Michael sees Judith at Christmas every year. Every year he brings her the same box of inexpensive chocolates. Every year she thanks him, gives him a hug and a kiss on the cheek. The last year she sees Michael is the year he returns her kiss with one of his own. He's drunk. He kisses his daughter full on the lips, his tongue forcefully finding hers, his hand finding her breast. Judith pulls away, tears in her eyes. She mouths, "Why?" Then she turns and runs into her house, locks the front door.

Her mother asks her if she is all right. Judith nods. The next Christmas when Michael knocks on Randy and Susan's front door, Judith refuses to come out of her room. All Susan can get out of her daughter is, "I don't have to see him. I won't see him. Tell him to go away."

Randy stands in the doorframe of his house. He says, "Mr. Lesser, you are no longer welcome here."

Michael threatens, but nothing comes of his words. Judith never sees her father again. Years later, she hears of his death from liver failure when the alcohol he loves so much finally takes him. He's only 52.

34 - BAD DREAM

When she remembers to answer, Annie tells Charlie many times that he isn't going to lose it. She promises. He doesn't seem to fully understand her; and the gap between sister and brother grows larger while Annie is in college. Annie spends her second year at Columbia University steeped in coursework, studying hard to keep her grades up. She and Linda stay together the second year by applying to live off campus in a small apartment. They have to share the bedroom and bath. For a while, the moments of communication with Charlie are far and few between.

One night, Annie wakes to Linda standing over her shaking her. "Wake up, Annie. You're having a bad dream."

Annie whispers, "A bad dream."

"Yes, you were screaming. Scared me to death."

Annie doesn't remember the dream. Still she figures it has something to do with a baseball striking her forehead.

"And you were talking in your sleep."

"I was?" says Annie. "What did I say?"

"I don't know for sure," says Linda. "Something about Charlie. He's your brother, right?"

Annie nods, says, "Makes sense."

"Anyway," says Linda, "maybe we should try to go back to sleep. We've both got early classes tomorrow."

"Yes," says Annie.

Annie hears Charlie, clearly. *That's good to know, Annie-belle. I'm so glad I'm not drinking. Thanks for letting me know. Thanks, little sis.*

Annie wonders, *Where are you, Charlie? When did I say all that?*

Annie sits on the edge of her bed, confused. She puts her head in her hands and listens closely to the dark. She doesn't hear Charlie. She waits, not moving. Linda stands beside her. She asks, "Are you okay, Ann?"

"I am. I think." She looks up at her roommate and debates whether she should tell Linda about the voice of her brother in her head. *She'll think you're crazy, Annie-belle. You know she will.*

Annie says, "Charlie?" Then realizes she says this out loud. Linda stares at her. Annie laughs, "It's okay, Linda. I'm still kind of asleep. Don't worry."

"All right," says Linda. "I won't. I'm going back to sleep. See you in the morning."

"Okay," says Annie. She stretches out and looks at the ceiling fan as it spins. The cool breeze blows against her face. She takes a deep breath and closes her eyes.

The baseball hits her squarely in the forehead; blood flows from her ears. She screams. *Hush, Annie-belle. You're okay. I promise. You aren't going to lose it.*

The next morning, Annie can't decide if Linda waking her is part of her dream. She determines not to ask. Instead, she and Linda make breakfast, then go to their separate classes. Linda starts a large new work in her oil painting class. Annie takes a particularly tough mid-term exam in biochemistry.

With a few other dayworkers, Charlie digs a ditch that morning in the heat of South Carolina, stopping on occasion for water. With each strike of the shovel, he remembers Annie-belle whereas Annie forgets Charlie in the meantime.

35 - VIETNAM VET

While Annie's away at Columbia, Rick struggles to find work. He is a disabled Vietnam Veteran in southwestern Ohio, and jobs are tough to come by, especially for veterans of the Vietnam conflict; and even more so for vets who are disabled. Rick is able to walk, but this is such a struggle. Mobility is easier in a wheelchair. He learns to stroke the wheels in such a way that he goes relatively straight and fast despite his right arm being weaker and shorter than his left.

For a few months, he wears his military uniform when he's out with Jim and Judith, but sees they are a bit embarrassed by - *is it me? or the uniform? or the war? or all three?* Instead, Rick puts on jeans and a brown leather jacket with fringe, and brown high leather boots reminiscent of cowboys and cattle drives. To top off his look, Rick wears a red and white paisley bandana around his head, tied in the back. In the bathroom mirror, Rick thinks he looks like a hood. *I'm not a hood; I'm a belated hippie. I'm a Vietnam loser.*

In the hallway, Judith stands behind the door to the bathroom. She peers at Rick, says, "You look like a pirate, Richard."

He laughs, "I do, don't I?"

"You better get out of that get-up before your father sees you."

Rick restrains himself, turns, says to his mother, "Yeah, you're right. Excuse me, Mom. I'm gonna go change."

Judith tells him he hasn't long. "We're leaving in five minutes."

"I probably won't make it then."

Judith shakes her head as Rick passes her in the hall. "Yes, you will."

"Okay," he says. *Still pushed around, hey buddy?* He struggles to the end of the hall, leans against the wall with his left arm holding most of his weight; he turns the door knob with his right hand and leans on the door so that his weight swings it open. He steadies himself and lurches through the door and limps across his dim room. He sits awkwardly on the side of his bed, spreads his legs so that his feet are firmly planted on the floorboards. He pants. *Well Mom I think that took most of your five minutes.* He laughs silently.

At the same moment, he hears Judith from the bottom of the staircase, "Richard. Come on."

He yells, "Coming, Mom."

Then he hears Jim. "Richard Logan! Get your ass down here now!"

Rick stands easily, having his feet spread and his weight stabilized. He limps to the door, locks it, limps back to the bed, sits. He waits. A few seconds later, he hears his father stomp up the stairs. *Here he comes.* The man rattles the lock, then pounds on Rick's door and kicks the bottom panel. Rick thinks the panel's going to pop out, but it doesn't. Judith is there a moment later calming her husband. *How does she deal with him so well?*

"Jim honey. He's not ready. Give him a few minutes."

"No, we're going." Jim spits his words like missiles. Rick hears him back away from the door, stomp down the stairs. The front door slams. Judith's steps are softer, but he hears her leave, too.

Rick sits on his bed, wonders momentarily what he should do next. He gets up, unlocks his door, sits and scoots down the stairs one step at a time, rises, gets his chair from the hallway closet, unfolds and locks it into position, pushes it outside to the front porch. *Time to wheelie down the front steps, Rick.* He puts on his leather gloves stored in a pouch on the back of the wheelchair. He sits, rotates the chair back onto its hind wheels, leans himself back and rocks onto the first step, balancing, balancing. Cautiously yet in a rush, Rick bounces down the four steps - one at a time - to the sidewalk. *Nothing! Nothing compared to having a mallet smash your knee!* He grins, wheels to the end of the sidewalk, turns right to head into Turtle Creek proper.

Rick has more difficulty negotiating the steps at the Methodist church. *No ramp.* Another late-comer helps him by carrying the wheelchair up to the front door while Rick struggles up the steps. He sweats all the way. The late-comer opens the door and he and Rick enter the sanctuary where Rick sees a good crowd. Individuals stand crowded together in each long wooden pew. They sing a hymn Rick vaguely recalls. He wheels to the end of the last pew, locks his brakes, glances at the lady next to him. She smiles, hands him her open hymnal, points to the line and the word. He nods, begins to sing. When the hymn closes, everyone sits except the minister who stands. Rick sticks out into the aisle, and is easily noticed by the man behind the podium.

"Why," the minister begins, "we have a hero with us today."

People stir.

Rick feels his face go bright red with blood. He shakes his head, glares at the man he also vaguely recalls. *What's this guy's name?*

"You all know Richard Logan," says the minister who, from this distance, is unable to see the expression on Rick's face.

People stir again, turn in their seats, look. The lady next to Richard beams at him, her eyes bright and kind.

Judith sees her son. "Oh lord, Jim."

Jim rises, pushes his way through the people to the end of his pew. He walks quickly to Rick, who unlocks his chair and backs up, swinging around to head to the door. Jim pushes the chair as soon as he reaches his son. Under his breath, he spits, "Bastard."

Judith politely says, "Excuse me" as she moves through the same people and out into the aisle. She turns toward the minister and points her finger at him. "You ought to know better than that," she says, surprising herself. She continues, "You ought to be ashamed."

The man looks at her with an expression of complete bewilderment.

Judith, Jim and Rick drive the Chevy truck home; the unlocked wheelchair rolls around in the truck bed.

36 - MISTER RIGHT

Annie becomes aware of Gary Holden at the beginning of her Junior year at Columbia University when he transfers in from Stanford. Annie sits next to him in physics. She notices him immediately. His beard is a rusty blonde and well cropped with a delicate mustache of the same color above his upper lip. His eyes are sharp blue. He stands six feet even and appears to weigh about one hundred and seventy pounds. Annie sees that his nails are short and clean. She likes this. When he smiles, his teeth are white and straight. *He's gorgeous.* She tells Linda all about Gary before she knows his name.

On Wednesday in physics, Annie sits beside Gary again. Today she leans over and extends her hand. "Hi," she says, "I'm Annie Logan. I'm a third year."

Gary looks at her briefly, says, "I'm Gary Holden. I'm a fourth year from Stanford. I transferred in."

"Nice to meet you," says Annie, smiling at him. He briefly returns her smile, looks distracted, goes back to the book open on the desk top in front of him. He stops, looks at Annie again. He appears to think for a moment, then asks, "Have you read this?"

Annie looks at the book as Gary closes it so she can see the cover. The book is *Shogun* by James Clavell. "No, I've not even heard of it."

"Just came out. Great book," says Gary. "I'll loan it to you when I'm done. If you'd like, that is."

Annie smiles. "Well, I don't know how you study and read long novels like that one at the same time."

"Got to," says Gary. "I'd go crazy if all I did was study mathematics and chemistry and biology."

"Yeah, I guess that makes sense."

The professor comes into the room, begins to write a formula on the chalkboard without addressing his classroom. Gary leans in close to Annie, whispers, "Want to get a cup of coffee after class?"

Annie smiles again, "Sure."

Gary buys Annie a cup of coffee during their first date. After that, Annie spends as much of her free time with Gary as she is able and still maintain her grades. Gary is very smart and doesn't seem to study as much as Annie. Later in the semester she discovers her grades are slightly better than his. *Maybe that's why he transferred. I wonder - Is Stanford harder than Columbia? Or maybe it's just that I work harder.*

Nevertheless, at the end of the following year, Gary graduates from Columbia on time. As she applauds for him, Annie is excited because Gary is admitted to the medical school of New York University; Columbia turns him down but no matter because he won't be far from her. She calms herself as she watches Gary walk across the stage to receive his diploma. *Medical school is a full time occupation.* Gary tells her this when he accepts NYU's offer. "Annie," he says, "I'm not going to have the amount of time you expect."

"I know," says Annie. "Just don't forget to call me."

Gary smiles.

In her senior year, Annie studies hard but Gary must study harder; she hears from him once a week and sees him on Sunday afternoons. Otherwise, their contact is sparse. Annie doubts the strength of the relationship, but when she is with Gary, all is right with the world. He's gentle and attentive. And, by the end of the second year with him, she is pretty certain he is in love with her as she knows she is in love with him.

Then, one evening somewhat late, Annie calls Gary with a study question. By now she's in her first year of medical school still at Columbia University. A woman answers the telephone. Annie hears Gary in the background, "Don't."

Annie says, "Who's this?"

Gary answers, "It's me."

"No, who is there with you?"

"John's girlfriend, Speedy is here."

"Speedy?"

"Yeah," says Gary, "that's what he calls her."

"May I speak to Speedy?"

"Why?"

"Why not?"

"I don't know," says Gary. "What's the point?"

Annie thinks about this. *He's right. I'm not trusting him if I want to speak to Speedy. Speedy? What a weird name.* "Okay, never mind." She pauses, then says, "Gary, I've got a problem here I can't figure."

"What is it?"

Annie tells Gary about the biochemistry problem, asks him several questions, listens intently to his answer. "Does that help?" he asks.

"Yes, got it. Thanks so much, sweetheart."

"Okay," he says somewhat abruptly. "I gotta go."

"Oh," says Annie. "Okay."

"Okay, goodnight." And the line disconnects.

Annie looks at the phone. She puts the receiver down and gets an overwhelming heaviness in her chest and stomach. She doesn't see Gary for several weeks, and he doesn't call her like he usually does. Annie picks up the phone a few times in those weeks to call Gary, but decides against it. When she finally sees him, he gives her a quick hug and a gentle peck on the cheek.

"I've missed you," says Annie.

"Yeah, I've been super busy."

"I'm sure," says Annie. "Me, too."

Gary looks at her. "Come here, Annie." She stumbles to him. He takes her full in his arms and holds her tightly. He says, "I'm out of time, Annie."

"What?"

"I can't do this anymore."

"What?" She tries to pull back so she might see his face, but he holds her tight and close to his body.

"I need you."

She laughs slightly, a laugh of relief. "Well, I need you, too."

"Good," he says. Then, he lets her go. Gary holds her a few feet from him, and looks her directly in her eyes. "Will you marry me, then?"

Annie starts to answer, but Gary puts his forefinger to her lips. "Wait. I need to tell you something first."

"What is it?"

Gary looks at his feet briefly, then back into Annie's eyes. He says, "I'm not going to be a doctor, Annie."

"What?" Annie is surprised.

"Yeah, I'm not making it."

"Oh Gary."

"Yeah, med school's been just way too tough for me. I can't keep up."

"What are you going to do?"

"That's the good news. I'm transferring into pharmacy school. I'm gonna be a pharmacist. I can do that. That's no problem."

"Is that what you want, though Gary?" Annie wipes a tear that suddenly falls from her right eye.

"Well, it's better than doing nothing with all my completed coursework in the sciences." He grins.

Annie stares at Gary, wonders how well she really knows him. He completely surprises and disappoints her with this news. She sits down on a bench, puts her head in her hands. She sees a baseball sailing up at her, feels it strike her forehead, knows blood is gushing from her ears. For a moment she hears Charlie's voice but can't make out what he says. She thinks: *Maybe I'm the one who's losing it, Charlie.*

Charlie says, *No Annie. Annie-belle, you're okay. You're not losing it. I promise.*

Annie sits on the bench, listening. The welt in the center of her forehead is not palpable. No blood gushes from her ears. She only has a terrible headache that throbs behind her eyes. She glances at Gary, who sits beside her. She asks, "So, when do you start?"

Gary confesses, "I already transferred."

"When?"

"Two weeks ago."

"Does this have anything to do with Speedy?"

Gary shakes his head, looks at her.

"Does it?" Annie asks again.

"Yes."

"What is it?"

"Speedy gave me the idea in the first place. She's a pharmacy student here."

"Really?"

"Yes, really."

"Okay." But Annie sits with heavy doubt. Gary takes her right hand, holds it gently. With his other hand, he moves her face toward his own and kisses her. She dissolves into tears. "I don't know what to think, Gary."

"It's okay, Annie. All this is a shock. I should've told you. I'm sorry."

"Are you in love with Speedy?"

Gary pulls away. "What?"

In the back of her mind, Annie recognizes the absurdity of her question, but she goes on with her line of thinking. "You heard me. Are you in love with her? What's her real name anyway?"

"I don't know her real name. She's just Speedy. That's what John calls her - Speedy."

"She's really John's girlfriend?"

"Well, of course!" says Gary. Annie knows he's suddenly angry. "What the hell, Annie. What? You think I've been cheating on you all this time?"

"I wasn't sure."

"Well you should know me better than that, by now!"

Annie nods. *He's right.*

Charlie says, *Yep Annie-belle. He's gotcha there. Apologize, you dimwit.*

"I'm sorry, Gary."

37 - THE PIRATE

As he gets into the Chevy truck outside the Methodist church, Jim screams at Rick, "What were you thinking? Coming to church dressed like that!"

Rick doesn't respond. He thinks of his landing on the surface of the moon, the bounce of his movement across the moonscape. He looks up through the thin atmosphere to the dark above, sees Earth floating out of his reach. Jim's voice is like fog, thick but distant. *What's the man saying?* Rick looks at his mother who sits between them on the bench seat of the Chevy truck. Judith stares out the windshield while Jim rants about the minister. Judith nods once. She looks at Rick, nods again. She says, "Stupid, stupid man."

"He didn't mean any harm, Mom." Rick is generous. He tries to be kind. "I don't think he knew how I'd feel. I mean, I don't think he knew that he would hurt us."

Judith sneers, "But he should know."

Jim returns to the subject of Rick's clothing and now focuses on his hair as well. Rick's hair is grown to shoulder length and his beard is full and ragged. "You look like -"

Rick interrupts, "A pirate. Right Mom? I'm a pirate."

Jim takes a hand off the steering wheel to reach passed Judith to attempt a strike at Rick's left leg. Rick blocks the blow, calmly protests, "No. Don't do that."

Judith says, "Yes Jim. Stop."

Jim strikes his wife instead. His blow lands on his wife's left shoulder. She looks at her husband with shock. Rick goes berserk. He grabs his father's right arm and pins it to Judith's lap. The Chevy swerves, and Jim instinctively brakes. The back end of the truck fishtails, and the left rear tire blows. The truck spins around and slides into the shallow ditch on the side of the road. Judith hits her chin on the dashboard as the truck comes to a stop. Jim is pushed into the steering wheel and sits groaning. Rick smacks his head on the passenger side window. No one loses consciousness. No one bleeds. From the truck comes a hiss. The three sit, watch steam rise from around the hood.

Rick says, "We should get out."

"What?" asks Judith.

"He's right," says Jim. "We ought to get away from the truck just in case."

Rick struggles to open his side door, and barely manages not to fall out of the cab of the truck. He lands on his feet, then sits down on the grass growing along the side of the ditch. Judith follows him, sits beside him. Then Jim gets out on his side, crawling against gravity. He walks around the truck for Judith who refuses to take his offered hand.

"No," she says. "I can do it myself." She pushes herself up from the ground and walks away from the truck. At the same time, the truck emits a mighty groan. Jim thinks, *Damn thing's farting at us.* Rick crawls out of the ditch, and moves to the back end of the Chevy to retrieve his wheelchair as quickly as possible. Jim realizes and helps. Together the two men get the chair out and down onto the ground. Since they didn't fold it when it was put into the truck bed, Rick sits in it and rolls away. Jim follows.

"Let's find a pay phone," says Jim. "I'll call a tow service."

The tow truck comes forty minutes later, and leaves with Jim's beloved Chevy within fifteen minutes. Then Jim, Judith and Rick take a taxi home, the wheelchair folded and placed in the cab's trunk.

No one speaks; the cab driver looks repeatedly at each one of his passengers in the rearview mirror. *He's wondering what's with us,* thinks Rick. Rick glances at his mother whose chin is swollen as well as black and blue. He feels his own head; a lump there on the right side above his ear and under his hair. The only apparently uninjured one is Jim. Sure enough, the cab driver stares at Jim who sits between Rick and Judith, looking severe.

38 - OTHER PARTS

Gary doesn't say he accepts Annie's apology and offers her no explanation. Annie waits. She looks at him intently but he refuses to defend himself. Instead, Gary stands to walk away. Annie remains on the bench. She calls after him briefly, but stops. She leans back, raises her eyes toward the sky and the clouds moving rapidly across its blue background. *Well I blew that.*

Annie does not see Gary for several weeks. He doesn't call her apartment. She does receive a small card with a tiny flower embossed on its front; inside a handwritten line that states, "Very busy. Will call you next Saturday. G." Annie turns the card over, stares at the Hallmark logo. She looks at the envelope; the return address is missing. Gary's handwriting is micrographic but legible. She doesn't notice the faded red postmark on the envelope.

Annie is lucky; like Gary she's also very busy with medical school. She works on a research project with a small group, studies for two exams, and writes a portion of a short paper due at the end of October. She shadows a resident M.D. at the hospital. Still, she thinks about Gary and wonders when she'll see him again.

On Saturday, as he promises, the telephone rings. Annie picks up the receiver. "Hello, this is Annie."

"Hey Ann."

"Gary!" The thrill in her voice is almost ridiculous. She calms herself.

"I want to tell you something."

Oh no. "Yes?" she asks.

"I want us to take a break."

Oh god.

"Ann?"

"I'm here."

"Listen. It isn't that I don't want to see you again. I do. I just need some time."

"To study?"

"Well yes," he says. "But it's more than that." He stops talking. She can hear him breathing hard.

"Are you okay?" asks Annie.

"Yeah I'm okay. This is just harder than I thought it'd be."

Annie takes a chance. She says, "Well that's because you should be telling me this in person."

"Oh," he says. "Yeah, I guess so. But..."

"But what?" Annie hears the anger in her voice. She adds a gentle tone: "What, Gary?"

"It's too hard to see you right now."

"Okay," she says, fighting tears. "Well, I think I know why. But, could you tell me?"

Gary doesn't speak.

"Gary?"

"I'm here."

"Well?"

"I can't," he says.

"Is it because of what I said about you and Speedy?"

"Yes, that's part of it."

Part of it? "What's the other part?" she asks.

"I can't," he says again.

Annie waits a moment, says, "All right. How long?"

Gary responds, "I think -" He stops. "I think maybe a few months."

Annie is shocked. "Months?" *You don't love me. You don't want me. Oh god.* She calms down again. "That's a long time, Gary. Are you sure?"

"Yes," he says. "I'm sure."

Annie feels anger. "Well," she says. "I don't think I want to see you ever again."

"Oh, don't say that, Annabelle."

"Why not?"

"Because," he says, "you love me."

Annie emits a sharp laugh, a "ha!" Then she bangs the receiver into the cradle of the telephone. The two hard plastic objects make a loud crack as they connect. Annie goes to her bedroom, stretches out on her bed, cries herself to sleep.

39 - AMERICAN FLAG

Jim nails a metal flag holder to the front porch, and sets the American flag out on Columbus Day. He looks at the sky. *No, it's not going to rain. Don't forget, buddy. Bring the flag inside if it starts to rain. The neighbors* - He stops. *Who cares about the Pissletons, anyway? Or the Mulhaneys, for that matter. Or the Carroways!* Jim turns, takes his hammer and goes back into his house. Judith sings in the kitchen. Jim tosses the hammer on the end table in the foyer; as it lands the claw dents the wooden top. *Shit.* He picks up the hammer, shoves it inside the little drawer below the top of the table. He spits on his thumb and rubs the scratch on the table; it darkens. Then, Jim walks into the kitchen.

"Where's Rick?" he asks Judith.

"I think he's upstairs in the shower."

Jim sits at the table. "Where's my coffee?"

"Here," says Judith. She turns, hands Jim a cup of hot coffee. He adds cream and sugar, holds out his hand. Judith notices, hands her husband a teaspoon with which he stirs the hot liquid.

A few minutes later, Rick appears in the doorway. Jim glances up. Rick wears a shirt made from an American flag. He wheels his chair into the kitchen, says, "Hey Mom. Dad." If he expects Jim to yell, Rick doesn't show this. He goes to the refrigerator, opens it, pulls out the orange juice, puts it on the counter next to his mother. He looks at her. She knows. She hands him a small glass from the cabinet above him. "Here," she says. She stares at his shirt. He looks down, then winks at her. She glowers.

"Rick," says his father.

"Yes," says Rick.

Calmly Jim says, "Go upstairs; change your shirt."

"No," says Rick. *I sound like a two year old.*

"No?"

"Yes." Rick looks at his father. "You heard me." *Or a defiant teen.*

"I did." Jim stands, walks to the back door and out into the yard, carrying his coffee cup with him. He stands in the yard.

Judith turns to Rick, "That's dumb, you know."

"What?"

"Challenging him like that."

"Don't you mean the other way around? Isn't it Dad who challenges me? I have to be just like him or he freaks out. I have to do everything he says, or he hits. He hits you, Mom." *Finally, a man. I sound like a man.*

Judith turns to the sink, puts her hands in the dish water. "No, he doesn't hit me."

"Now that he doesn't have Charlie to kick around, he sure does hit you."

Judith shakes her head. Michael, her father, flashes before her. She looks over her shoulder at her son. "No, Rick. Your father doesn't hit me."

"What are you smoking, Mom?"

Judith doesn't recognize this expression, so she just giggles.

"What are you laughing at, Mom?"

"You, Rick." She turns, claps him on his left shoulder with her soapy wet hand. "You're so serious." She grins, dries her hands on her apron, walks out of the kitchen, through the back door to stand next to her husband.

Jim doesn't look at her, but asks, "Will he change?"

"The shirt, you mean?"

He smiles at her and nods.

"Yes, if you leave him alone; let it be his decision. But as for *changing*, no I don't think so. Not without some help."

Jim shakes his head in agreement. "I think you're right, sweetie. I think you're always right."

"Most of the time," says Judith and hugs her husband. He holds his coffee away from his wife's body and hugs her back with one arm.

40 - SOMETHING TERRIBLE

Rick climbs the stairs slowly with great effort, goes to his room, changes his shirt. *That was damn silly.* He looks in the mirror. His hair is shoulder length and tangled. His beard is ragged. He pulls a pair of small scissors from the medicine cabinet, leans in close to the mirror, much of his weight on the bathroom sink. He begins to trim his hair, cautiously at first then quickly. Hair piles up in the sink. Rick takes toilet paper from the roll, wets it, and sops up the hair to toss into the trash can by the door. Next he attacks his beard, clipping most of it off before shaving with Ivory soap lather and a razor. Soon, his face is baby soft. He trims the mustache, leaves it neat. His hair looks pretty awful, but he doesn't care. *At least it's short.*

Rick goes downstairs, sits in his wheelchair, rolls out onto the back porch. He watches his parents for a few minutes. Jim has an arm around Judith's waist and Judith leans her head against his shoulder. *They look very young from this angle.* Rick clears his throat. Jim turns.

"Hi Dad," says Rick.

When his mother realizes her son can't get down the back porch steps easily, she walks over to Rick. Jim follows his wife.

Rick says to his father, "I'm sorry about the shirt."

"That's okay," lies Jim. He is about to comment on his son's hair when Rick speaks first.

"I'm feeling lost," says Rick. "I feel like I'm 13 again."

Judith nods. *He's beginning to see it.*

"I don't seem to have any direction."

Judith nods again.

"I'm just lost." He looks at his mother. "I'm a lopsided man."

Jim stares, obviously bewildered. But Judith smiles, comes close to her son and gently rubs the top of his head. "That's okay, Richard. I'm glad you realize what's happened."

Rick looks up at his mother. "What's that mean, Mom? What's happened?"

"Something terrible," says Judith.

"Terrible?" asks Rick.

"Yes," says Jim, suddenly following his wife's line of thought.

"What?" says Rick, looking back and forth between his two parents.

"Torture," says his mother. His father nods, tears forming in his eyes.

"Torture?" asks Rick, now the bewildered one.

"You remember," says his father.

Rick sees the moon dust kick up under his boot, float in the thin atmosphere for what seems like minutes then slowly fall back to the ground in front of him. He bounces again, reaches up to touch the planet Earth. He shudders.

"I remember the trip to the moon," says Rick.

Judith looks at Jim, whispers, "Easy."

"The moon?" says Jim.

"The earth's beautiful from there, you know."

"I bet," agrees Judith.

"But," continues Jim, "you remember what happened outside Hanoi."

"The Hotel?" says Rick.

Judith nods. "Yes, Richard, the hotel."

"I remember the Hotel was dirty. I remember the scratching." Rick's hands shake and he involuntarily taps his right foot against the foot rest of the wheelchair. "I remember hunger. I remember being hungry - always."

"Do you remember how you got the scars on your chest?" asks his mother.

Rick shudders again. The earth seems to fall toward the moon, filling the dark sky with its ever enlarging circumference of blue and white and tan. *Run. Run. Run.* Sweat pours from beneath Rick's arms and beads up on his chest. He licks his lips; his tongue is dry in his mouth, sticky. *Lord, I'm thirsty. How do I get out of this? I need to run. But my legs are heavy like logs.*

Rick looks up at his mother, "Mom?"

"Yes, honey."

"I feel like I'm going backwards in time. I thought I was 13, but I'm feeling like I'm even younger than -" His voice cracks. He looks as lost to Judith as he seems to feel.

"That's okay, darling."

"But Mom," protests Rick, "I shouldn't be here."

"Where should you be?" asks Jim.

"On the moon, Dad. I belong on the moon."

41 - NEW ARRIVAL

Zach taps, "I can't get the guy next to me to respond, Rick."

"Maybe he's dead."

"God, I hope not," says Zach. "I'm so ready for some outside news."

Rick leans against the wall, and laughs. *News. I wonder if anything on the evening news is different from this. Is this all Walter Cronkite is talking about?* He says, "Keep trying."

"Oh I'm not giving up. I mean, the guy just got here. Maybe he's terrified of me."

"Hell, I'm terrified of you and I've been here as long as you have."

Rick hears the muffled laughter of his friend through the thin wall.

Several days later, Zach taps: "Got him. His name's Jake Johnson. What a name! He's from Berea, Kentucky wherever that is."

"Has he seen any movies this year?"

"Yeah, I asked. I thought he'd never tell me! You won't believe it!"

"What?"

"Jake says some movie came out that's about a guy trying to escape all the stuff about this war - you know, all the protests. He goes to live with his wife who's British. They wind up in her hometown, and the townspeople, I guess, are horrid to him and wind up gang-raping his wife - shit - one of their own even! Anyway, he's like a pacifist, but he goes nutty and I guess kills them all. He kills each one in some special, really brutal way."

"What's it called?"

"Just a sec," says Zach. A few moments later, he taps, "Jake says it's called *Straw Dogs*."

Rick says, "Never heard of it." He can hear Zach's laugh. "You better be careful with that laugh of yours. I can hear you through the wall. You'll have the gooks on Jake and you and me if you're not careful."

"Yes, Mommy. I'll be careful."

Turns out Jake Johnson is in the war only a little longer than Rick when he's captured by the North Vietnamese. He's older than Zach and Rick, and cautious. Communication with him proves difficult. He's what Zach refers to as "closed-mouthed."

"He's a tough nut to crack," he says to Rick. "He told me he lost a brother here last year."

"Here?"

"In this war, dummy."

"Gotcha."

"And his sister's a nurse in Saigon. He's not heard from her since before he got here."

"Here?"

Zach laughs, taps, "In Vietnam, dummy."

Rick closes his eyes, feels the nurse touch his cheek. Her eyes are so black, so full of -

The lock clicks. Two men appear in the doorway. Rick opens his eyes. "Welcome home, guys."

When Rick is returned to his cell, Zach taps but gets no response. He tells Jake, "I'm worried about my best pal, Rick. The gooks kept him longer than usual."

Jake responds with "Don't worry" which Zach takes as a euphemism for "I don't care."

Fourteen hours later, Rick responds to Zach's now frantic tapping. He says, "I'm alive. The gooks smashed my other knee - that's all."

"They waited until your right one was about healed up."

"That's right," taps Rick.

"Why'd they keep you so long?"

"Oh," responds Rick, "I passed out and they kept throwing ice water on my face. They'd bring me back, then stomp on my knee so I'd pass out again. Went on like that for hours. It was just hours, right? Not days?"

"No, not days."

"Thank goodness."

"We're making Jake nervous," says Zach.

"I imagine so."

Zach asks if he's eaten, but Rick doesn't respond. Zach waits.

In his cell, Rick's eyes close and his breathing deepens. His back rests against the wall, and he dreams of his descent into a deep crater on the moon's surface. Earth disappears behind the crater's rim as Rick loses his footing and tumbles into the dark. Buzz Aldrin's voice comes over the com: "Richard Lewis Logan. Richard. Over." Rick can't answer. He falls through the thin atmosphere, reaches up toward the night sky and the stars strewn across it.

42 - DON'T FUSS

Charlie wakes Annie, *Don't fuss, sis.*

What?

Don't fuss, Annie-belle.

Trying.

Good to hear. Then, Charlie asks her what he usually wants to know. *Am I losing it, Annie-belle? I feel like I'm losing it.*

Like she always does, she encourages her older brother. *No, Charlie. You aren't going to lose it.* Then she promises. She always promises. And Charlie always seems to believe her promises.

Annie goes back to sleep. As she relaxes, she thinks of Gary. But her overwhelming concern for this moment is her brother, Charlie. *Where are you, Charlie? Why aren't you playing baseball? What'd you do with your catcher's mitt? I couldn't find it.* No answer comes to her mind as she falls into sleep.

In the morning, Annie goes to the hospital in her short medical student white lab coat, pages the chief resident. She's instructed to perform a thorough chart review and come up with some preliminary orders. The challenge focuses Annie on herself and the patient. Both Gary and Charlie fade from the forefront of her mind. She spends the first hour of her morning perusing handwritten medical records and making tough decisions as quickly as possible after she examines an elderly female patient sustained by a large ventilator with tubes and wires emerging from all parts of the body. The chief resident checks in before 9:30, speaks with Annie, examines the same patient with her as she stands by.

"Okay, tell me about Ms. Greenberg."

Annie runs through the lady's history and current condition including all the signs and symptoms she is able to recall. At this point, Annie realizes she's taken poor notes and scolds herself. To the chief resident, she speaks of a general plan of care, then gives several specific suggestions otherwise known as orders.

The chief resident nods. "Sounds good to me, Ms. Logan." He turns to the chart, opens it, finds the order page, and scribbles the orders that Annie recommends. He signs his name. As he writes, Annie marvels at the M.D. at the end of his signature. *One day. One day.*

The rest of the day is busy, and Annie gets home exhausted and hungry. Linda surprises her with dinner on the table. "Oh my goodness, Linda!" says Annie. "You are such a doll. Thank you."

Linda opens a bottle of red wine; it's cheap but tastes of black cherry and licorice and is delicious in the opinion of both women. Linda serves it with saltines and an equally inexpensive cheese. Neither of the two young women has excess money, so cheese and wine, no matter how lowbrow in cost, are luxuries. They enjoy their evening briefly before Annie excuses herself to study. Linda nods, raises her glass, says, "Go for it, Annie."

Annie smiles, and goes to her bedroom. There, she sits at her small desk and cracks the books, again.

In the middle of the night, Charlie wakes Annie. *What is it, Charlie?*

I'm scared, Annie-belle. I don't have enough to eat. The lice and mosquitos are getting more of my blood than I'm getting food to eat. And I can't find anything to drink. I got the shakes, Annie. Real bad. I'm losing it. Annie. I know I am.

Charlie, you're not losing it. I promise. I've got to get a full night's sleep. Please stop waking me up. Please, Charlie.

No response. Annie tries to relax, but worry overwhelms her. *Where are you, Charlie? What's going on? Why won't you go home? Go see Mom and Dad.* Annie listens, but her mind is silent. The remainder of the night Annie's sleep is restless, shallow, dreamless. She wakes in the morning with a horrid headache. She figures the headache is from the cheap wine. She drinks several cups of coffee to wake herself before going to her first class. In the afternoon, she goes back to the hospital. The chief resident tells her she looks ill.

"I'm not sick," says Annie. "I'm not sleeping well. That's all."

"Well that's good," says Dr. Lancaster.

Annie nods. *It's good that I'm not sick, but I've got to sleep well tonight.*

She calls her parents long-distance collect that evening. She speaks to her mother, tells her about her dreams of Charlie. She doesn't tell Judith that she actually hears Charlie's voice in her head; she figures her mother won't understand that. *Who would understand that, anyway?*

Her mother says, "You poor thing, Annabelle. Try to let go of Charles. I don't know where he is. Your father searched Atlanta for any sign of where he might have gone from there. He found nothing, absolutely nothing. I think we've got to accept that we've lost Charles to some force of evil. I don't know what else to call it. He's gone. He's just up and gone." Annie hears her mother's voice break.

"Oh Mom, I'm so sorry. I should've kept my mouth shut. I'm sorry."

"No, honey; it's all right. You have to express your feelings or you *will* get sick. Just try to get some sleep. Try not to worry about Charles."

"Yes ma'am."

"Good-night, sweetheart."

"Good-night, Mom."

As she sits on the edge of her bed in the dark, Annie remembers playing hopscotch with Charlie. Rick refuses, but Charlie draws the big hopscotch board in chalk on the sidewalk running along their street in the front yard. Charlie tosses the rock, hops forward. He coaches Annie when it's her turn. She squeals, delighted when her toss is better than her older brother's.

Annie shakes her head, stretches out on the soft mattress, eventually sleeps fitfully. When she wakes in the morning, she hears Charlie, *Don't worry about me, Annie-belle. I'm lost. Mom's right.*

43 - THE LETTER

At the end of her day, Annie opens the envelope she finds in the apartment mailbox in the downstairs hallway. The envelope has no return address, so she thinks it may be from Gary Holden. When she unfolds the two page letter and begins to read its first page, she smiles. The letter is from Gary.

Dear Ann,

I'm really sorry I didn't tell you I was dropping out of medical school. I don't know how you got the idea that I was in love with John's girl, but that's water under the bridge. I think John's going to marry Speedy. I wish I knew her real name so I could tell you what it is. But I don't. Anyway, you need not worry about Speedy; she's not in the picture for me. She was just someone who made a good suggestion for me.

I'm really liking pharmacy school. It's right up my alley. And I'm doing very well, too. So that's good. I should graduate next summer, and be able to get a job right away. Everyone says the market is good for pharmacists. So, that's why I'm writing to you now.

I am thinking that once I graduate, maybe you and I can get married. I guess this is an odd way to propose marriage - again! - to a girl. But I can't think of any other way to do this right now since I can't come to see you. I bet you are wondering why I can't stop over and give you a big kiss. The reason I can't stop in to see you is that I am not in New York. And it's not just the city either. I'm not even in the state. I bet you didn't look at the postmark on the envelope. Did you? I bet you didn't. That's just like you, Ann. You miss the little things, don't you?

Annie stops, picks up the envelope. Sure enough, the postmark is not of New York, but of California. She goes back to the letter.

I'm in San Francisco, studying here at UCSF; that's University of California, San Francisco but I bet you knew that!

I miss you so much, Ann. Won't you be my wife? You can write your answer to me, if you will. I don't have a telephone or believe me, I would have called you by now!

Love always, Gary

Below his closing salutation is his address. She struggles to control her tears. She has so many questions. She picks up her stationary, and a nice pen and begins her reply.

Dearest Gary,

You are right about me. I didn't look at the envelope at all because as usual you didn't put a return address. I have so many questions that this is probably going to seem like an interrogation.

First, why California? And do you plan to live there? Second, why do you want to marry me? You haven't seen me in six months! How can you be certain? Third, can you wait for my answer until we can see each other in person?

Oh this is so difficult to do on a piece of paper. Don't you have enough money to call me from a pay phone? Maybe you've forgotten my phone number.

Annie writes her telephone number in the body of the letter and some good times that he can call her. She reminds him that she's three hours later than he is in California. She writes that she still loves him, and that she's seriously considering his proposal. Then she signs the letter, addresses and stamps the envelope, almost runs to the mailbox to drop it in the outbox.

Then she returns to the apartment and takes a hot shower, dresses in her softest pajamas for an early bedtime. She's so tired and so excited.

44 - THE SUNRISE

You're a beautiful bride, Annie-belle.

Annie wakes with a start. *Oh gosh, Charlie. You scared me.* She listens in the dark as usual but hears nothing more. She goes back to sleep.

The telephone rings in the living room. Annie struggles from under the bedcovers, kicking them out of her way. She hurriedly exits her room, goes into the hallway, then to the table where she finds the phone still ringing. She picks up the receiver. "Hello?"

"Ann!"

"Gary!"

"Can you talk?" he asks.

"Oh yes. Sure." She sits on the couch, leans back, takes a deep breath.

Gary asks, "So are you doing okay?"

She laughs. "Well sure. And you?"

"Well, I miss you tons."

"I miss you, too."

"So, do you want to marry me?"

"Gary," pleads Annie. "Slow down."

"What?"

"I need to see you."

"Well," he says, his voice tinny over the distance, "I don't know how we can make that happen until I graduate and come back to New York."

"So, you are coming back here."

"Well, of course."

"Gary, that's not been clear to me. Well, not until now."

"Well, Ann you've got to finish medical school and your residency. Right?"

"Exactly."

"So, it follows we'll live in New York, in the city."

Annie sighs with a relief even Gary picks up over the phone line. He says, "I'm sorry. I assumed you knew that."

"Well I know now. And it's good to hear that's your plan."

"Always has been," says Gary. "I didn't know how to tell you after you hung up on me that day."

"Yeah, I'm sorry about that. I was pretty upset."

"I realize that -"

A woman's voice tells Gary to deposit $1.35 for two additional minutes. Gary says, "I don't have any more money, Ann. I'll write -"

The line goes dead. Annie hangs up the receiver and closes her eyes. She stays on the couch for a few minutes before going into the kitchen to get a glass of water. Then she goes back to bed, but can't sleep. She stares at the ceiling, and waits for the morning light to enter through the window blinds. *As soon as I see the sunrise, I'll get up.*

45 - SAFE HERE

As Jim and Judith once direct a young Charles to Alcoholics Anonymous for help, now they direct Richard to a psychiatrist at the University of Cincinnati School of Medicine. Rick resists only briefly, then nods his head when his mother expresses her concern privately and with tears. He says, "Okay, Mom; I'll go."

Jim, Judith and Richard drive the Chevy truck from Turtle Creek Township to Cincinnati. Rick navigates with the open map in his lap.

"Turn here, Dad." Jim turns the truck into an alley leading to the hospital parking garage. He parks, steps out, helps Richard into the wheelchair. The three of them go across a connecting ramp into the hospital lobby. They are directed to registration where Richard fills out several forms before settling down to wait.

A woman in a lab coat calls his name after fifteen minutes. He wheels over and follows her into a separate unit on the same floor of the hospital.

"Wait right here." She points to an alcove with several couches and tables with magazines lined up neatly on them. Rick wheels over, locks his brakes, leans over, picks up a men's magazine, glances at its cover, tosses it back on the table. He looks around. Only a few other people wait. One is a young woman staring straight up at the ceiling. Another is an elderly man twiddling his thumbs over and over.

A few minutes pass, then the woman comes back. She motions to Rick which surprises him. He follows her. She opens a door in the hallway, says, "Wait here. The doctor will be with you shortly."

He doesn't wait long in the little room before a knock is heard against the doorframe. The door opens immediately and the doctor enters.

The short man with a greying beard and thinning hair says, "Hello Mr. Logan. My name is Dr. Scott Matthews." He extends his hand which Rick takes, reaching out with his shorter right arm.

"Hello," he says. "I'd stand up, but that's tough to do offhand like this."

"That's not an issue Mr. Logan. You may stay seated where you are comfortable."

"Comfortable," repeats Rick. "That's funny."

Dr. Matthews raises an eyebrow. "Is it?"

"Yes," says Rick.

Dr. Matthews sits on a rolling stool next to Rick. "Really? Why is that?"

"I'm hardly comfortable in this chair, Dr. - what's your name again?"

"Dr. Matthews."

"Oh, right. Dr. Matthews. Yes, I'm hardly comfortable in this wheelchair."

"Well Mr. Logan. That was only an expression."

"Oh really. Okay. Whatever you say."

Dr. Matthews hesitates, then says, "I guess we've gotten off on the wrong foot here."

"I guess so," says Rick.

"Well," says the doctor, "what exactly seems to be the problem?"

"Problem?"

"Uh," says Dr. Matthews. He looks at the intake sheet on the clipboard in his lap. He reads a few sentences, glances up at Rick. "I see you're a Vietnam veteran."

"Yes," says Rick.

"And a prisoner of war, too."

"So I'm told."

"How was that?"

Rick laughs. "How was that? What do you think, doc?"

"I've no idea. Tough, I'd imagine."

"Yes, it was tough."

"Okay. So tell me about it."

Rick looks at the man. He shakes his head.

The doctor waits. He waits for several minutes for Rick to speak, but Rick doesn't offer anything. "Okay," says the doctor, "is there anything you want to tell me?"

Rick shakes his head, "No, not really."

"So, may I ask why you are here today?"

"You may ask."

"Come on now," says the doctor, "You might give me a break."

Rick smirks. "Yeah."

"So there is something to tell me?"

Now Rick hesitates before he responds, "My mother worries about me."

"Why is she worried?"

"You'll have to ask her," says Rick.

"Back to your old tactic, hey?" says Dr. Matthews. "Okay, I'll ask her." He leans over, pushes a black button on a small box. A voice comes over the speaker, "Yes sir."

"Would you ask Mrs. Logan to join us."

"That won't be necessary," says Rick.

"Never mind," says the doctor to the intercom. He turns to Rick. "So?"

"I was a prisoner of war. I know that, but I don't remember it." He waits, examines Dr. Matthews.

Dr. Matthews pauses, then asks, "And do you dream about the war?"

"Not that I know. I never wake up, you know, with - you know, I don't have nightmares. I guess that's what you mean."

The doctor nods. "Yes, that's what I mean. So, no nightmares, no flashbacks?"

"No, not really," says Rick. "I remember something that *can't* have happened." He stops.

"What's that?"

Rick laughs nervously.

"Don't be afraid to tell me. If it sounds crazy, I mean. It's okay. You're completely safe here."

Rick nods, but doesn't respond. After waiting in silence for three or four minutes, Dr. Matthews tells Richard that's enough for today. Then he tells Rick he'll need to come back.

When Rick returns to the lobby of the hospital, his mother asks, "How did it go?"

"A bit touch and go at first, but I think it went well overall."

"That's good," says his father who claps him on the shoulder. "Let's go home."

"Yeah we can go home but you need to know," says Rick, "I think the doc would very much like to admit me."

"No," says Jim immediately. "No, that's not happening."

"Dad," says Rick. "I'm an adult. If I agree, you can't stop it from happening."

Jim sinks onto the couch. "Please don't do this. Come on home with us. Didn't that doctor give you some medicine or a shot or something?"

"No," says Rick. "He thinks hypnosis is going to help me. I need to remember what happened to me over there."

Judith nods. She turns to Jim, touches his knee. "This is important, Jim. We need to support our son in this. Okay?"

"All right," says Jim.

Under his breath, Rick whispers, "Thanks, Dad."

Jim either doesn't hear his son or ignores him. "So," asks his father, "you aren't being admitted today, are you?"

"I don't think so, Dad. I've got to go home, get some stuff for my stay."

"Good," says Judith. "Let's go home then."

The drive back to Turtle Creek is quiet. Judith keeps reaching back to touch Rick's knees, first his right then his left, patting them the way she pats him when he is her firstborn. He's a beautiful baby boy, pink all over and hefty. He is born with his eyes wide open, hands outstretched, not crying but looking all around. Even the doctor seems surprised at his vigor and curiosity.

"That's quite a man you've got there, Mrs. Logan," he says when he stops by her room in the maternity ward of the hospital later in the morning.

"Thank you Dr. Hanson. Thank you so much for everything."

"It's my pleasure, Mrs. Logan. Believe me." He points to Richard who sleeps in his mother's arms. "Look at him. He's beautiful. You must live right."

Now, Judith looks at her crippled son, her lopsided man. *Odd that Richard refers to himself that way - as a lopsided man.*

Once home, Rick packs a small suitcase with underwear, several tee-shirts, two pairs of slacks, an extra pair of shoes, his toothbrush, brush, comb, razor, and a small collection of toiletries. He puts the suitcase on the floor of his closet, and crawls into bed. As he begins to drift into sleep, he discovers tears on his face. He cries, but he doesn't know why. He wonders about Charles, where his little brother might be and what he is doing. He thinks about Annabelle, too. He imagines her as she studies medicine and wishes her good luck. He turns over, pulls his knees to his chest and surrenders to sleep. *Soon I won't be as lopsided. Soon.*

46 - NO CHAMPAGNE

Gary moves back to New York City when he graduates from University of California at San Francisco. He obtains a license to practice as a pharmacist and easily finds an entry level job for a drugstore in Brooklyn even before he lands at the airport.

When he arrives, Annie splurges. She takes a taxi to LaGuardia to meet Gary at the gate. As he comes into view, she sees him as he towers over the people around him. She almost screams, "Gary. Here, Gary."

He pushes passed several people carrying luggage, and runs to Annie's arms. She hugs him; he hugs her and deeply kisses her. "Oh Ann. I've missed you so much." They stand, holding each other tightly, both crying. "Oh Annabelle," Gary repeats. "Gary, Gary," says Annie, burying her face in the shirt covering his chest.

He pulls away from her, holding her at arms' length. "So, you're gonna marry me. Right?" And with that, he drops one knee to the floor and holds out a small black velvet box. Annie takes the box, opens it. Inside is a white gold ring with a single small diamond. Gary rises, takes the box from Annie, pulls the ring from its holder, and reaches for her left hand. He slides the ring on her finger, and looks at her. She looks at the ring, then at Gary. She smiles. "Yes, Gary. I'll marry you."

People watching begin to applaud, one at first, then everyone who stands around the couple. Gary laughs; Annie blushes. Gary speaks to the small crowd, "Show's over, folks." Then, he takes Annie by her shoulder and guides her away from the people still standing around them. "Come on, honey. Let's go."

Gary and Annie catch a taxi that takes them back into Manhattan. They get out early to save a little money, and walk four blocks to Annie and Linda's apartment. Annie says, "This is it. This is home. Come up and see Linda."

Gary stares at her.

Annie realizes. "Oh, Gary. I'm sorry. You need to sleep here, don't you?"

"Yeah, if it's okay."

"Sure, you can take the couch. Linda won't mind."

"Thanks, honey."

"You're welcome," says Annie, laughing. "I'm just sorry I didn't figure it out earlier."

Linda is in the kitchen cooking when Gary and Annie come in. She calls out, "Hey girl."

"Hey Lind," says Annie. "You remember Gary."

"Oh yeah. Hey Gary."

Gary nods, then speaks to Annie. "I'm gonna use the facilities, if that's okay."

"Of course. Here, let me take your suitcase. I'll put it in my room for now." Gary opens it, pulls out his toiletries, hands his luggage to

Annie, and goes down the hallway. Annie calls after him, "Third door on your left, Gary."

"Thanks."

Annie says, "Be right back, Linda." Linda nods. Annie takes the suitcase into their bedroom, sets it by the window, comes back into the kitchen. She says to Linda, "Gary's going to spend the night. Okay?"

"With us?" And Linda nods her head in the direction of their shared bedroom.

"No, of course not," says Annie. "He's gonna sleep on the couch."

"Sure thing," says Linda. She grins.

Annie holds out her left hand. Linda is busy stirring the rice that has finished cooking. She adds a pat of butter and stirs again.

"Look, Linda."

Linda glances at Annie, who wiggles her left hand. "Oh, Annie!"

"Yeah!"

"So, he asked you all formal like, hey?"

"At the airport!"

"At the airport," says Linda. "That's wild. And you said yes?"

"I did!"

"So did you two set a date?"

"Not yet."

Linda puts down the spoon, and hugs Annie. "Congratulations! I'm so happy for you."

"Thanks Lind."

Gary comes into the kitchen, gives Linda a quick and friendly peck on her cheek. "Hello Linda."

"Hi Gary."

"Thanks for having me."

"I'll set another plate," says Linda.

"No, I will," says Annie. And she opens the cabinet to retrieve a dish for Gary. Then she gets out silverware and a napkin, places all on the table for him.

Linda says, "Hey that's a nice ring you got for Annie."

Now Gary blushes. "You like it, hey?"

"Definitely," says Linda. "Congratulations! Too bad we don't have any champagne."

47 - CHECK IN

Jim takes Richard into Cincinnati to the hospital for check-in at the psychiatric ward. Rick thanks his father, then quickly says good-bye. He doesn't linger, but turns, enters the locked unit with the help of an attendant and without looking back. His father stands in the lobby for a few minutes, then leaves to drive back to Turtle Creek Township. He finds Judith sitting on the porch steps, head in her hands. She looks up as Jim walks up to her. "So, is he okay?"

"I think so," says Jim.

"How long will he be there?"

"No one spoke to me at all," says Jim. "I've got no idea."

"I can't," says Judith, "lose both of my boys, Jim."

"Of course not," says Jim, sitting down beside her. "You won't. I promise."

"At least Annabelle's doing well."

"Yep," says Jim. "Our little girl's gonna be a doctor."

"Amazing, isn't it?"

Jim chances it, says, "Yep, both our boys need doctors and our girl turns out to be one."

Judith laughs. Jim sits relieved that his wife's sense of humor remains intact.

Judith says, "Yeah, but Charles never got the help he needed, did he?"

"Not that we know, Judy."

She repeats Jim, "Yeah, not that we know."

Richard Lewis Logan signs in as a voluntary commitment. As he signs his name, his right hand shakes and the formation of his letters looks miss-aligned and incorrect to his eyes.

"Come with me, Richard."

In his wheelchair, he follows the tall lanky woman down the hallway and into a large common area. The ceilings are high, and the noise level is intense. The woman leaves Rick with a nurse who asks him several questions that he can't fully answer. She shows him his room which he shares with another older man. The man is in the bed. All Rick sees is the top of the man's head which is covered with white bushy hair and a small crooked cap. Rick looks at the rest of the room. His twin bed is against the other wall and is covered only with a thin white sheet. No blanket. The pillow looks rock-hard. The walls are a light blue and completely bare. There's only a single large overhead light; no lamps on the two end tables which also function as dressers. Rick sighs. *Not much better than a prison.*

Rick meets with Dr. Scott Matthews within an hour of arrival, and this reassures him. His first and lingering impression is that he's made a terrible mistake admitting himself to this ward. *This place is depressing!* But Dr. Matthews knocks on Rick's door, opens it, nods. Rick smiles. "Come with me, Mr. Logan."

"Gladly," says Rick.

"Did you get settled in?"

"Somewhat," says Rick.

"Can be difficult at first," says the doctor.

"I guess so."

"Are you ready to get started?" asks Dr. Matthews once they are seated in his office. Rick says he is ready.

Rick looks up after a few minutes, "So are we going to start soon?"

Dr. Matthews smiles, "We've just finished."

"We've finished?"

"Yes, you've been under hypnosis for thirty-three minutes." Dr. Matthews points to the clock. "I just woke you."

"How come I don't remember?"

"Because that was my suggestion, that you not remember this first session."

"Why?"

"Some pretty awful things happened to you in Vietnam, in that prison. I think we need to ease you into those memories not bombard you with them."

"Makes sense, I guess."

"Well, the fact that you don't remember much of anything from those years means we should tread carefully."

"So, what happened to me, doc?"

Dr. Matthews asks, "Do you recall anything?"

Rick says, "I remember being hungry all the time, and being afraid of starving to death."

Dr. Matthews nods. "Anything else?"

Rick says, "No, nothing."

"Well," responds Dr. Matthews, "you've got to know that they broke both your kneecaps."

"I guess so," says Rick.

"Do you know what they used?"

"No, I don't." Rick's hands and his right leg begin to shake slightly. Rick puts his left hand on his right thigh and pushes. He grins at the doctor. "That's so weird."

"It's okay, Richard. May I call you Richard?"

"Call me Rick."

"Okay Rick," says the doctor. "They used a large mallet with a steel head, from your description."

"Oh god," says Rick.

"Yeah," admits the doctor, "that's what I said, too when I heard you describe it."

Rick feels sweat beading up along his hairline, and abruptly asks if he can leave. The doctor says that of course he can go. Rick returns to his room, and tries to sleep.

His roommate, the older man with white bushy hair, chants throughout Rick's first night. Rick can't make out if the man's chanting contains real words that form a prayer or if it is only nonsense syllables, disconnected sounds without meaning. Nevertheless, Rick finds the chant haunting. He lies in the darkness on his hard mattress with his head on the equally hard pillow. *I've felt this way before. But when? Where?* Rick realizes he misses his mother. He knows he's felt this before.

The next day at the second session Dr. Matthews asks Rick, "Do you remember anything pleasant about being a prisoner of war?"

"Pleasant?"

"Yeah, you know - anything nice. You know, relatively nice compared to the misery you don't remember."

Rick waits. *I can't remember anything.*

"Do you remember a hospital?"

Rick shakes his head. "No, I don't."

"A woman?"

Rick lowers his head. He doesn't remember a face, but he sees a straw hat, broad-rimmed and black eyes. He shakes his head, but verbalizes what he sees in his mind.

"So, you remember a hat and black eyes?"

"Well, I see them." And again, he's shakes; sweat pours from his armpits. "I can't," he says. "I can't."

"It's okay; just breathe."

"I can't breathe," says Rick. He suddenly realizes he's lost control of his urine. "Oh oh," he says. "That's -"

Dr. Matthews is right there. He helps Rick from the wheelchair and into the restroom. He leaves Rick on the toilet while he uses the intercom on his desk to request hospital scrubs for him. An attendant brings them a few minutes later. Rick pulls off his wet slacks and places them in a plastic bag Dr. Matthews provides - he pulls it out of the bottom of the trashcan for Rick. He also gives Rick adult wipes, apologizing for them at the same time.

"No, that's all right," says Rick. "I'm the one who should be sorry."

"No, fear is a powerful thing, Rick."

"Yeah, I guess so."

"Come on out whenever you're ready."

Rick sits on the toilet and cries. He leans forward and uses a wipe to clean the seat of the wheelchair then dries it with toilet paper. Then he swings himself back into the chair and wheels back into the office where Dr. Matthews waits.

"Hello Rick. Are you okay?"

"Hello Dr. Matthews. Yeah, I'm okay."

"It's nothing to be ashamed of."

"If you say so."

"Yeah, I say so."

Rick glances up at the doctor. Dr. Matthews smiles.

During his fifth session with Dr. Matthews, Rick screams in the middle of his hypnotic trance, and Dr. Matthews wakes him.

"Oh god!" says Rick.

"What?"

"I remember being stabbed by a soldier with a bayonet. And there was a girl."

"A girl in the prison?"

"No, in a hospital. I think she may have been a nurse. Maybe."

"So, you were kept in a hospital?"

"For a little while, I think. I had a broken arm."

"Of course," says the doctor. "Your right arm is shorter than your left because of the way your shoulder and upper arm healed after multiple injuries."

"I was hurt when our Huey helicopter was shot down," says Rick. "We were under heavy fire and the engine failed. We dropped out of the sky. The Viet Cong were all over us in just a few minutes. I remember being in so much pain that I could hardly stay conscious. But they were coming across the field, running to us. Then I must have passed out cause the next thing I remember I woke in a cell with a dirt floor and straw everywhere and a scratching sound all along the far wall."

"Rats?"

"I've got no idea. In the three years I was there, I never saw the things that made all that awful scratching noise."

"Really?"

"Really. I remember when I woke up, I found out only four of us survived the crash. Oh -"

"What?"

"Zach!"

"Who?"

"Zachary was our crew gunner; he was in the cell next to ours."

"Ours?"

"Oh -" gasps Rick. "Oh, Bob. Bob was my co-pilot. He didn't make it. They - oh god - they tortured him. They beat him to death."

Rick sobs, shakes. Dr. Matthews stands, comes close, holds Rick's left shoulder tightly. "Just breathe." Rick continues to cry, the tears roll from his eyes, collect in his lap. Dr. Matthews squeezes Rick's shoulder tighter. Rick takes several deep breaths and stops the tears. He looks up into the doctor's face. The man appears warm, caring, engaged.

Dr. Matthews asks, "Do you remember anything else? Anyone else?"

"Two men; sometimes three."

"Prisoners?"

"No, guards." Rick gasps again. He stutters, "And, And an electric outlet hanging above me; it was connected to a heating iron of some kind."

"Is that how you got the burns on your chest?"

Rick shudders as the memory floods back to him. Dr. Matthews squeezes Rick's left shoulder harder, and commands, "Breathe, Richard, breathe." He squeezes the young man's shoulder again, tightly. "Need to stop?"

"Yes, yes - I need to stop. Let's stop, please."

"Okay. You're going to completely wake up Rick when I count to six."

Rick interrupts him, "I thought I was awake."

The doctor raises his eyebrows, continues, "As I count, with each number, you are going to feel more and more at peace and less and less disturbed by your memories. When you are fully awake, you are going to remember everything you told me today and nothing more about your captivity. Okay, ready?"

"Ready."

Dr. Matthews counts to six, slowly and steadily. As he does, Richard Lewis Logan relaxes. By the count of six, he smiles at the doctor who says, "Okay, that's it."

"Okay," says Rick. He sits in his wheelchair, waits. He shakes his head. He looks at Dr. Matthews with wonder. He says, "I remember Zach and Bob. I remember the hot iron. I remember the soldier with the bayonet and the beautiful young nurse who was so kind to me. I remember the helicopter crash. I remember everything."

Dr. Matthews smiles, lies, "That's great, Richard. I'm glad your memory is back."

48 - INDEPENDENT GIRL

I wish I could be there, says Charlie.

Annie's engagement to Gary is long. Annabelle insists that she finish medical school before she marries. And, she refuses to live with Gary or sleep in the same bed with him until her wedding night. She's terrified of getting pregnant especially before her medical degree is earned but also before her residency is finished. Of course, she realizes that once they are married, she'll sleep with her husband and will need to use great care to keep from becoming a mother before her plans call for parenthood.

Gary grudgingly tolerates the long wait. He spends many hours at the pharmacy, compounding drugs and counting out pills for acutely ill or chronically ill people who come to the drugstore where he works. He takes advantage of the wait time, saving money for his upcoming marriage to Annabelle Logan.

In many ways, the two avoid each other. Often Gary finds being close to Ann very frustrating. He doesn't fully grasp her desire to wait until the wedding night even though he's certain his parents do and he imagines Annie's parents do as well.

The sexual revolution is rampant in New York City, all around the couple. To delay what Gary often considers inevitable, he and Annie go on formal dates. When he can, Gary picks Annabelle up outside her apartment, takes her out on the town, returns her to her apartment door. When he can't pick her up, they meet at a public location or event, spend the evening together, and part outside her apartment or on the subway platform. Gary rarely comes up except occasionally to eat dinner with Annie and Linda.

Gary and Ann are seldom alone and together at the same time. Gary believes Ann is used to being on her own due to his time in California. *She's an independent girl. Wish I knew how to be that independent.* He misses her so much when he is not with her; his hours are more open to boredom and loneliness than hers. *She has studies to keep her occupied. I've only got her.*

Annie reserves weekend days for study, choosing to go out on Saturday night only. Gary sometimes expresses anger over not being able to see her on Friday night.

"What am I supposed to do tonight?"

"I don't know, Gary. Go to a movie. Go see *Rocky.* I heard it's pretty good."

"Come with me," he says.

"I can't, Gary. I've got to study. You see it. Tell me what you think tomorrow night."

He sees *Rocky* by himself, and is fairly impressed with Sylvester Stallone's writing and acting. He tells Ann how good it is. She says, "Well, we can see it next weekend; maybe Saturday night."

Gary shakes his head, "I don't want to see it twice, Ann."

"Oh, okay. Sorry."

"And with as little time as we get to be together, I don't really want to spend our time in a dark movie theatre where we can't even talk."

191

"Sure," she agrees. "I don't want to do that either."

The next year and a half is the same for Gary and Ann. Gary continues to work as the chief pharmacist in the Brooklyn drugstore; Ann graduates from Columbia University's School of Medicine and starts her hospital residency. Initially, exactly as she dreams since childhood, signing her full name followed by the capital letters M.D. thrills her. Unlike her childhood dream, rather than treat children, she doctors adults.

Charlie says, *I wish I could be there, Doctor Annie-belle.*

I wish you could be here, too, Charlie.

49 - WEDDING WISH

Judith and Jim invite Gary into their home, putting him in the back bedroom near the downstairs half-bath in the hallway. Even though Judith teases him about it being bad luck to see the bride on the day of the wedding, she allows Gary to sit at the kitchen table with Annie, Rick, Jim and herself for an early breakfast. She serves scrambled eggs with cheese, bacon, toast and fresh fruit. Gary is complimentary as he devours everything on his plate. He keeps smiling at Annie, squeezing her left hand which she rests in his lap under the table.

The wedding is set late in the afternoon at the Methodist church where Jim and Judith return despite the episode with the preacher and Rick. The man calls on the Logan household several days after that Sunday, ringing the doorbell, waiting on the porch for Jim to come to the door.

"Mr. Logan, good evening."

"Good evening, sir." Jim struggles, but can't remember the man's name. "Come in, won't you?"

"Yes, please." He extends his hand. "I'm Pastor Salkmon."

"Pastor Salkmon, yes. Come on in." Jim leads the gentleman into the front room and points to the couch. "Have a seat. I'll let Judith know you're here. I think she's in the kitchen."

"Okay, I'm fine."

Jim finds Judith in the kitchen. "Come on," he says. "Pastor Salkmon is here. He's in the living room."

"Oh crap," says Judith.

"Judy!"

"I'm sorry. I'm not sure I'm ready to see this man."

Jim takes Judith's hand and guides her into the living room. Pastor Salkmon looks up, stands, smiles, walks to Judith and gives her a quick hug. Then, he returns to sit down on the couch.

"Would you like something to drink?" asks Jim.

"No, no." The man smiles again.

"Well, in that case," says Judith, "what can we do for you?"

The pastor pats the couch beside him. "Come sit here, Mrs. Logan."

She hesitates, but sits.

The man turns to her, takes her hands in his. "I apologize for Sunday. I had no idea that Richard would react that way. I was just trying to honor him and soldiers like him."

Judith tears up.

"Oh don't cry," says Pastor Salkmon. "I came by to tell you both how sorry I am for what I did and for what happened to Richard in Vietnam. What a terrible time that young man had."

194

"Yes," says Jim. "His experience there was terrible. We accept your apology, sir. Thank you for taking the time to come by and tell us this."

The pastor stands, shakes Jim's offered hand. "Well, it is the least I can do. I hope we'll see you in church this weekend."

I wish I was there, says Charlie to Annie-belle as she dresses for her wedding.

I wish you were here, too Charlie. How I wish it.

At the Methodist church in late spring with flowers in full bloom, Pastor Salkmon asks Gary Lucas Holden if he takes Annabelle Louise Logan to be his lawfully wedded wife, if he plans to have and hold her from this day forth, for as long as they both shall live. And Gary says, "I do." Then the pastor asks Ann the same thing except he asks her if she plans to obey her husband. Annie hasn't thought about this part of her vows, so easily responds, "I will." Then she smiles, blushes, and says, "I mean, I do."

"Do you have the rings?"

Gary takes the white gold wedding band from his breast pocket, takes Ann's left hand, slides the ring on her third finger. Annie takes the yellow gold wedding band she's clutched in her hand throughout the ceremony and slides it on Gary's ring finger of his left hand.

"I now pronounce you man and wife," says Pastor Salkmon. To the man, he signals, "You may kiss your bride." Gary lifts Ann's veil and kisses her gently.

The entire church membership stands, applauds.

I'm sorry I can't be there, Annie-belle. I'm so sorry.

Annie ignores Charlie, walks down the aisle with her new husband, out into a fine rain that's more akin to mist. Her father provides an umbrella so she and Gary remain essentially dry as they climb into the car. "Thanks, Dad. See you at the reception."

The reception at the Logan home is very small: Richard, Jim, Judith, Robert and Hanna Holden who are only able to come in on the day of the wedding; Gary and Annie, Annie's bridesmaids, Betty Sue and Mary from high school, and the maid of honor, Linda, Annie's best friend from New York; Tommie Feldon, Gary's best man and Marcus Wooten, a good friend from Gary's California days.

Judith caters the meal at Jim's insistence. "No need to work yourself into the ground, Judy." The mid-evening meal is delicious and Judith is glad she listened to her husband. Tommie toasts first, then Linda. Everyone drinks champagne. Annie and Gary cut the cake, share the first piece with one another.

While everyone else is eating cake, Annie slips from the table, goes upstairs, changes into her honeymoon outfit - a light blue matching jacket and skirt; comes back down, joins the rest in the living room while the caterers clean up the dining area. Gary beams when Ann comes into the room. She smiles at her husband, gives him a quick kiss on the cheek, sits beside him. He says, "You look beautiful." She grins.

"So, where are you two going?" asks Linda.

"Tonight," says Gary, "is a surprise. Tomorrow night we head out for Chicago. We've only got a few days, so we'll make the most of our time."

"A surprise?" says Linda.

"Definitely," responds Annie. Robert Holden winks at her, raises his champagne glass.

The surprise is extraordinary in Annie's experience.

Later that evening, Annie tosses her bouquet which is caught by Betty Sue even though the newlywed aims for Linda. She and Gary then say their good-byes; and Gary drives their rental car into Cincinnati, down to the edge of the Ohio River to park outside Riverfront Stadium. Annie looks at the round building, then at Gary.

"What?" She stares at her husband. "You're kidding."

"Come on," he says, taking her by the hand. He grabs their two suitcases with his other hand, one under his arm and the other clutched by the handle. "Come on; wait until you see this."

He takes a key out of his right pocket, and opens a gate, locks it after they pass through. Then he takes Annie into the open area of the stadium; as he enters the field he flicks a switch in a box along the wall. A single row of lights comes on, casting a beam onto the artificial turf. Annie sees the baseball diamond in the far corner of the round stadium. She speaks softly, "Charlie."

"Excuse me?" says Gary.

"Nothing," says Annie.

"Come on," says Gary, like a child.

She follows Gary. He leads her up an aisle into the bleachers. She has to stop a few times to catch her breath. "Come on," he urges her. They go all the way to the top and then Gary comes to another door. He uses the same key - a master key - to open this black door with PRIVATE written in white paint across its front. Gary enters, flicks on a light switch. Annie looks around. She knows where she is. A large couch and several smaller chairs line a glass wall to her left facing the field below. A bar with a refrigerator and sink and a counter with stools line a wall to her right. Straight ahead is a bathroom and a small closet. Next to the closet door is a large double bed.

Annie laughs, "Oh Gary, we're in the owner's box."

"Yeah," he says. "Isn't this cool?"

"But how?"

"My dad," says Gary, "is a good friend of the owner of the stadium."

"So, we're spending our first night here?"

"Yeah," he says excitedly.

Charlie says, *Too bad I never got to play Riverfront.*

Annie shakes her head. *One for you, Charlie. God, I wish you were here.*

Annie sits on the black leather couch facing the baseball diamond dimly lit below. She cries for her brother who, despite his childhood dream, never plays with the Big Red Machine. Her husband stands behind her, hands on her shoulders. He says, "I know; it's kind of an overwhelming sight, isn't it, Ann?"

Annie nods, then turns to Gary. She stands close to him and begins to unbutton his white dress shirt. He grins, kisses the tears from her eyes and cheeks while he fumbles with his own belt before he stops to start on Ann's neckline - the black round buttons on her blouse are tiny and Gary is awkward. Ann is completely inexperienced and Gary suddenly worries he'll scare or even hurt her. But Annie's willing to help. Soon they are both undressed and together in the same bed for the first time in their long relationship.

Much later, stretched out on the bed in the owner's box above Riverfront Stadium field, Annie stares at the ceiling tiles and the fan that quietly spins above her and her sleeping husband. She sees a blue bicycle with an older man riding it. *Is that you, Charlie?*

Not yet, Annie-belle.

Where are you, Charlie?

I don't know how to tell you, Annie. But, I know I'm alive.

That's good, Charlie.

What I never seem to know is if I'll lose it or not. Am I losing it, Annie?

No, I don't think so. I don't think you'll lose it, Charlie.

Can you promise?

Annie hesitates. She's not certain she knows what Charlie is afraid to lose. She tries to ask him but he never answers this question; it's as if he can't hear her when she asks. The ceiling fan clicks as if one of its blades is repeatedly striking something hard in the air. She says to the dark, *I promise, Charlie. You won't lose it. I promise.*

Charlie doesn't respond; Gary snores. Annie cuddles up against her husband and laughs at their surroundings. *Who would plan to have their honeymoon night, their wedding night in a baseball stadium?*

50 - THE BUSKER

A few days after his arrival by bus to Columbia, South Carolina, Charlie meets a street musician named Tammy who plays pots, pans, colanders, wood blocks, whistles, spoons, and a washboard all connected to a large tricycle with a drum attached. Tammy rides around downtown Columbia near the University of South Carolina, banging her instruments via pedals in a manner pleasing to Charlie and to many others. People pay her to play. Charlie is amazed at how much money passersby drop in her coffer.

Tammy lives in a tent in the central park of Columbia right off the square where the capital building stands. The police harass her sometimes, but she thinks because she's a woman, they cut her some slack. They bug her until she takes down her tent, but ignore that she puts it back up in a slightly different location within the park.

Charlie meets her by hearing her music coming from the other side of the park. He follows the sounds, and finds her seated on her tricycle banging away. He sits on the edge of the sidewalk to listen. She notices him, stops playing, comes to sit beside him on the sidewalk edge.

"Hi," she says.

"Hey," says Charlie.

She introduces herself; he does the same.

"So Tammy, are you from Columbia?"

"Nope," she laughs. "You can't tell?"

Charlie shakes his head.

"I'm British, born and bred in Manchester." She smiles, her teeth are black here and there. He looks away. She says, "And you?"

"I'm from Ohio."

"Cold!" She laughs.

"I guess so," says Charlie. He remembers the short summers more than the long winters. He remembers spring practice on the baseball diamond at school and glorious summer days with Rick, playing catch. *Rick*. He gets no response from his older brother. He never does.

"What is it?" asks Tammy.

"What do you mean?"

"I don't know. You just stared at me for a few seconds, like you took a nap, went out for a long lunch, or something."

"Yeah," he says, matter-of-fact. "I do that."

"Look through people?"

"Yeah, right through 'em."

"Eerie."

"I've heard that, too."

She grins.

"I like your music," says Charlie, changing the subject.

"Thanks. I do, too."

"You manage to make a living?"

"Oh, enough for food. Not enough for a place to stay."

"Still, that's pretty good."

"Right," she says, grinning again.

Charlie hooks up with Tammy for a few months. What Tammy discovers within the first day is that Charlie is a reformed drinker. She buys him a beer that first evening at a local bar off the square. Charlie wants another, and Tammy says, "No, honey; not on me tab." Charlie is sweet; doesn't get angry or even insistent. He gets sad, moody, lonely-like. He stops talking to her except to tell her he's fallen off the wagon and he's so sorry. That night, he sleeps outside her tent on the ground, his head curled up on his jacket, his arms wrapped tightly around him against the chill of the early spring air.

Tammy tells him the next day, "This is the beginning of my good days. I make most of my money in late spring and early summer. So, if you wanna hang with me, that'd be fine."

Charlie is surprised. *What can I do for her?* Tammy seems to read his mind, because she says, "You can help me watch out for the coppers. Help me move the tent. Help me scout out new places to busker."

Charlie laughs. *Yeah, sure.* He is certainly agreeable to this plan even though he's not sure he fully understands Tammy. Nevertheless, Charlie follows Tammy around downtown Columbia, helps her fix her tricycle once when a back wheel is flat, scouts out a few neighborhoods she's not visited. Mostly, he keeps company with her, figuring she's as lonely as he is.

Tammy continues to buy beer for Charlie. He asks her for one no more than once a week. Then, one day, he craves liquor. He's outside a bar. A woman who has too much to drink stumbles out onto the sidewalk. She bumps into Charlie. The odor of alcohol overwhelms him. His stomach knots up, and his mouth actually waters. He moves away from the drunk woman as quickly as he is able, but it's too late. The hunger, the thirst is full-blown. Charlie finds Tammy, begs her to buy him a hard drink in the same bar. She denies him. Charlie ignores that; he tells her he prefers gin. Tammy walks away from him. But later, she surprises him again. She buys Charlie a bottle in a brown paper bag. Tammy buys the cheapest stuff she can find, winces as she watches Charlie suck the gin down like it's water to a man dying of thirst.

Then, Charlie passes out. When he wakes, nursing a horrid hangover and headache, he weeps. He weeps from shame. He spends several years in North Carolina and in Ohio attending Alcoholics Anonymous with two great sponsors. When he leaves Toledo, he's sober. Now, he betrays his sponsors and himself. *I'm sorry, Jake. I'm so sorry, Scott.* He apologizes even to himself. Tammy puts his head in her lap and whispers, "There, there."

When Charlie's lucid, he decides to part ways with Tammy. Her money makes it too easy to buy alcohol. *Maybe that's the main advantage to being unemployed - no money for booze. What an irony! I've got to half-starve to keep sober!* He sets his sights on the Atlantic Ocean. *Either I can head to Myrtle Beach or maybe I can go down I-26 to Charleston.* Charlie decides to hitch a ride to Charleston, the holy city on the ocean.

51 - HOME PLATE

The next morning, Annie and Gary rise to the sun striking home plate. A little later sunlight creeps toward the pitcher's mound. Annie points, says, "My brother stood there."

Gary looks down into the stadium. "Where? On the pitcher's mound?"

"No," says Annie. "There behind home plate. Actually he crouched there."

"Rick?"

"No," she says, glancing at Gary, then looking him straight in the eyes. "My brother, Charlie."

"Your brother is a catcher for the Reds?"

"No, not for the Reds. He's - well, he was a catcher for the Toledo Mud Hens, you know, the minor league team for the Detroit Tigers."

"Yeah, I'm familiar with Toledo. I mean, I know where it is."

"Yeah," she says, "Charlie played for the Mud Hens for almost five years."

"Really? That's cool," says Gary. Then he asks, "Where does he play now?"

"I don't know."

"You don't know?"

"Yeah, I'm not even sure he's playing for anyone. We can't find him."

"Can't find him?"

"No, he disappeared from Atlanta a couple of years ago, and we've heard nothing from him or about him since then."

"Gosh," says Gary. "You know, I don't think you've ever mentioned your brother Charlie to me."

Annie raises her eyebrows. *You've got to be kidding. How can that be?* But, she says, "I've not?"

"No, not that I recall."

"Well, I'm surprised." *Considering I think about Charlie all the time, even on my wedding night and now on the first morning of my honeymoon, of my marriage.*

Gary asks, "So, did he play for Bobby Cox?"

"Who?"

"You know, the Atlanta Braves. Did Charlie play for the Braves?"

"I don't think so," says Annie. "But, I really don't know."

"Well, it's not too hard to find out. We just need to check the team roster from a few years back. He'd be listed if he played for them."

"Hey, he would, wouldn't he?"

"Sure."

"In fact," Annie says excitedly, "Charlie'd be listed for any team he was catcher."

"Of course."

"Oh my goodness," says Annie. "Maybe we can find him."

"I don't see why not."

"Unless," says Annie, "he's not playing for any team."

"In that case, it could be tough. Even impossible."

"Still, worth a shot don't you think?"

"Absolutely, honey."

"Oh Gary. To find Charlie would be so -" And Annie briefly tears up on Gary's shoulder. She raises her head, looks up into his face, and says, "I'm so sorry. This is our honeymoon and I'm obsessing on my brother."

"Yeah really," laughs Gary, "you're such a blubbering idiot, Ann."

Annie throws her arms around Gary's neck, peruses the owner's box at Riverfront Stadium and says, "Thanks so much for a memorable first night. You are one creative quirky funny man, and I love you!"

"I love you, too, Ann." Then Gary looks around the owner's box and says, "Maybe this wasn't such a great idea."

Annie blushes.

"If I'd known -" continues Gary.

"It's definitely not your fault, Gary. I should've told you about Charlie." *I'm still shocked I've not even mentioned him.*

"Why didn't you?""

"I've got no idea," she says. *Maybe Charlie, you can tell me. Are you a ghost? Are you alive? Will you ever say good-bye or come back to say hello?* She gets no word from Charlie.

Annie turns to Gary, kisses him. "This was super fun. Let's not worry about whether it was the right thing or not. It is what it is."

Gary nods. Annie says, "Let's go to Chicago."

52 - FINAL SEASON

Charlie crouches behind home plate his final season of minor league play, and watches his life fly by in the exact manner a baseball spins in to his glove. The life he sees is a flash and a blur, and he nearly falls backwards as the images - thousands of them - rush over him. He can't make sense of many of them, but during the flash and blur, one image stands out.

He sits at the back of Turtle Creek's Methodist church in the front row of the second level overlooking the entire congregation. At the altar is Annie-belle and a handsome man dressed in a pin-striped dark grey, almost black, three piece suit. Charlie's mother, Judith sits below him on the left with his father, Jim. His father wears a dark suit with a bright blue tie; his mother dresses in a pale peach skirt and jacket with white shoes and a peach colored hat. And Rick - *oh my heavenly Lord!* - sits next to them on the pew. Charlie recognizes the back of Rick's head.

Charlie yells, "Rick!"

Rick doesn't turn. Charlie tries again, "Rick! Yo, Rick!"

No response. A wheelchair is parked off to the side of the pew near the outer wall under a gorgeous stain-glass window of Jesus carrying a lamb over His shoulder. Charlie silently asks, *Rick? Rick? Is that your wheelchair? Are you hurt? What happened?* There is no response from Rick. So Charlie asks Annie-belle, who peers over her shoulder briefly, looks Charlie directly in the eyes and lifts her finger to her lips. Charlie stops talking to her at that moment, but then: *Oh Annie! You're getting married! This is your day, Annie-belle.* Again, she peers at him with a bit of a glare in the look, and lifts a forefinger to her lips. Charlie obeys his baby sister.

The pop fly baseball hits the dirt at the edge of the fence behind him, and the batter takes off after dropping the bat near Charlie's feet. A few seconds later, the umpire calls the runner 'safe!' at first base, and Charlie is disappointed that despite scrambling for the baseball, he misses it. He kicks the dirt around home plate, looks out into the stadium. Something doesn't seem right. People in the stands look strange. He stares. Their faces are all the same color - a sort of pale fleshy pink but these faces have no eyes or noses or mouths. They're blank egg-shaped faces without expression. Charlie looks at his feet, looks back into the bleachers. The people are all the same. *They're mannequins - faceless mannequins.* Charlie raises his eyebrows even as the hairs along the nape of his neck stand straight up.

Charlie hears Annie, *I don't know what they are, Charlie. I've no idea what this means. Please Charlie. You're going to be okay. You aren't going to lose it. I promise.*

Charlie looks again at the blank faces, and for the first time doubts Annie's promise. *You're a wonderful sister and a beautiful bride Annie-belle; but I don't think you should promise me - well - anything.*

Annie doesn't realize she's not hearing her brother very well. She responds quietly but firmly, *Charlie, I'm at my wedding. Would you please -* She sounds like she's guilty of something, but Charlie highly doubts this is true. Annie is an innocent. Of this he is close to certain. Although Charlie doesn't speak to her again, Annie continues: *Just try to stay still until I can get out of this fancy get-up and concentrate. Right now, I'm not supposed to be listening to you. I'm supposed to be listening to the pastor and to my groom. Oh Charlie, please.*

Charlie nods, stays quiet throughout the remainder of the wedding and the reception, speaking again when Gary shows Annie the owner's box at Riverfront Stadium and the Big Red Machine's baseball diamond. Charlie looks around the stadium and at the baseball diamond. *What a wonderful place.* He puts his glove to his face, smells the combination of sweat and leather. *What a fabulous life.*

Charlie picks up the baseball, throws it back to Steve, the Mud Hens' pitcher. Then Charlie crouches behind home plate and waits for the next batter to take his place. Charlie concentrates, gives Steve the signal for this pitcher's extraordinarily nasty fast pitch. Steve nods, winds up, lets the baseball fly. The batter swings; the umpire calls the first strike as the baseball lands in Charlie's glove. The batter looks at the catcher, then back to the pitcher. The second pitch; the second strike. The batter looks dejected. Charlie smiles. He chances a gaze to the crowd in the bleachers. These people he knows; they are not faceless, but screaming: "one more; one more." He signals to Steve who pitches a curve ball. Charlie waits for the baseball, glove hand ready.

In the distance - at the other end of the stadium, Charlie notes an older man who stands at the very top of the stands, cradling a blue bicycle. The man wears an open jacket, a black and red plaid shirt and a pair of khaki slacks. *Annie asked me about you. Are you me?*

Not yet.

The baseball - big as the moon - comes out of the darkness, strikes Annie full in the forehead, knocking her down. The grass is soft, the ground hard. Charlie kneels beside her; he cries. Annie laughs, then wonders why this dream is so funny.

The umpire yells, "Strike Three; you're out." And the faceless crowd is on its feet. From the crow's nest, the older man with the blue bicycle waves. Perhaps the man gives Charlie a thumbs up signal. Charlie's not certain; but he waves back. As Charlie waves, the older man transforms into his older brother, Richard. Charlie realizes. *I'm not catching. I'm at bat.* He looks at the bat in his hands. The baseball streaks by him. He drops the bat and stands like a little boy lost. He vaguely hears Coach screaming.

Suddenly, a batter from the opposing team swings as the baseball spins toward Charlie; the bat connects with the ball which sails over Steve, passes the short stop to land in the outfield. No one is there to catch it. The batter runs to first base where the umpire yells, "Safe." Charlie shakes his head, bewildered. Coach screams from the sideline.

Annie gets up off the ground. She brushes grass off her long white dress. Little green smudges don't come away. She laughs again. *What's so funny? Why am I laughing?* Annie searches the bleachers for Gary. She's sure he's in the stands, watching her brother play for the Toledo Mud Hens. *What am I doing in Toledo?* Annie doesn't see Gary, but she notices the older man with the blue bicycle as he waves. She follows the direction of his stance and wave, and sees the catcher behind home plate. *Oh my god, it's Charlie.*

Annie waves, happily yells, "Charlie! Charlie!"

Charlie looks up, distracted by Annie's voice. He can't see her, but he hears her. The man with the bike disappears the way a heat wave apparition vanishes when the car approaches it on a hot asphalt highway. Charlie looks again, but he never sees Annie. He picks up the baseball, throws it to Steve. Charlie crouches behind home plate, readies his glove once again as he does so many times before.

The older man says, *Never again, Charlie-boy. This is it. This is the last time. Take notice.*

53 - THE LOATHING

"Hey doc."

"Welcome back, Rick. What's it been? Three weeks?"

"A little more than a month actually," says Rick.

Dr. Matthews directs Rick to park his wheelchair in front of the desk.

Rick says, "I've started having really horrid dreams."

The doctor nods his head. "That's good, Richard."

"Is it?"

"Means you're starting to remember everything."

Rick admits, "I'm not sure I want to remember everything."

"Who can blame you?"

Richard stares at the doctor for a few seconds, then goes on, "I wake up in a cold sweat, a sweat I remember. It's especially bad under my arms, across my chest and between my legs. I drench my poor mother's sheets. I'm glad to be back at home, but - Shit, they had to buy a plastic mattress cover; the old cotton one just wouldn't do."

Dr. Matthews chuckles, then asks, "You said 'a sweat you remember'?

"Yes, I know that sweat. It comes when I'm terrified - I mean terrified beyond words. Do you know that feeling?"

"I'm blessed to be able to say that I do not."

"Yeah," says Rick, "you're lucky. The terror that brings that on me is - well, impossible to describe. It isn't even what they are going to do to you that's terrifying; it's knowing something is coming, something terrible and you can't stop it and you can't prepare for it. Well, you can try to prepare but -"

"No, Rick. You're correct. You can't be prepared for it."

"Yeah, it's so much pain and then the fear adds to the pain -" Rick glances up at Dr. Matthews, checks the man to see if he's listening, if he still cares. The man now leans in toward Richard. Sometime while Rick speaks, the doctor moves from behind the desk to sit on its edge directly in front of Rick's wheelchair. Rick can touch the doctor, he realizes, if he wants.

"Yes?"

"The fear multiplies the agony. And all the self-talk in the world doesn't change how much what they do hurts the body."

"What about in here?" And Dr. Matthews touches Rick's chest briefly.

"You mean my soul?"

"Your soul, your spirit - sure."

"I'm pretty tough, Dr. Matthews -" Then Rick stops talking. He looks up at the ceiling and fights the tears that well up in his eyes. He waits, then struggles to speak. "You'll never guess -" He sobs. "You'll never -"

The doctor stands, places both hands on Rick's shoulders and leans his weight into them.

Rick laughs between sobs, "I know - breathe!"

Dr. Matthews laughs, too. "Yep, it's key."

They both laugh, then Rick says, "Okay, okay. You can let go now."

Dr. Matthews releases his grip, sits back on the edge of the desk.

"What I am trying to say," says Rick, "is you'll never guess what hurts most."

"Probably not," says the doctor.

How can he possibly know.

"When I get drafted and called up, my little brother Charlie is my very best friend. We're like three years apart in age, and you'd think I would avoid him, but I don't. Instead we spend lots of time together playing catch. I pitch; Charlie catches. We do this for years and years. My Dad starts pushing Charlie around when he's just - maybe 3 or 4 years old. He wants Charlie to be a great batter or pitcher. Dad never thinks about Charlie being a catcher. Of course not. When Charlie can't bat, Dad gives up on him - not just baseball mind you, but everything. Charlie's just no longer worthy of his time, his love - of anything but my Dad's anger. And Dad's got plenty of that."

"Do you know why?"

"Something about my grandfather -" Rick stops, checks Dr. Matthews again.

"Go on," says the doctor.

"Yeah," says Rick. He stops again, looks out the window, continues, "Anyway, Charlie's a natural with a baseball glove. He can catch just about any ball pitched, popped, bunted - well, you name it; Charlie can catch it. He's amazing behind home plate. That's where he belongs. Well, I get drafted and sent to Vietnam and as you know within a month, I'm dead."

"Dead?"

"Yeah, I'm declared 'missing in action' but the air force reports me essentially as 'dead' to my family. It's devastating. Charlie falls apart."

Dr. Matthews waits, asks, "What do you mean, Charlie falls apart?"

Rick explains, "My little brother drops out of school. Well, first he starts drinking. He can't stop. Mom tells me he can't help it."

The doctor nods, says, "And *this* is what hurts the most?"

Rick shakes his head, "Almost." Rick's voice breaks; he looks into his lap, drops his head down as the sobs begin again. This time, he can't stop. Dr. Matthews waits again. Rick gradually regains composure, begins to speak, "Almost, doc. Almost. What hurts so much is I never see Charlie again. And Charlie has no idea I am alive."

"Oh, I see."

"There's more," says Rick.

"Okay," says the doctor a bit sheepishly.

"Charlie plays for two minor league teams. I never get the opportunity to see him play professionally." Rick sighs, pauses.

"Those gooks cheat me of that! I hate them so much; I hate them! They ruin my life, and they ruin my little brother! They totally mess with my little brother, Charlie. I hate them so much; it's hard to contain the amount of hatred I hold in my heart."

Rick's eyes glisten. He's doesn't cry now; he looks at Dr. Matthews with all the anger he's ever felt anywhere at any time. The man who sits on the edge of the desk, inches from Richard's broken knees, gasps. Before him, the young man in the wheelchair is nearly unrecognizable as Richard Logan. His eyes are slits; blackened with loathing. His lips are curled in what might be described as a permanent snarl. Dr. Matthews rises from the desk to retreat to the chair behind it.

"Richard, I'm going to count to ten. As I count you are going to fall into a deep sleep. You will hear me, but for the time you are asleep, you will not be able to speak. You are going to breathe slowly, taking in deep deep breaths and letting as much air out as you possibly can before taking another breath."

Dr. Matthews counts. Richard glares at the doctor. He says, "Not gonna work, doc."

Dr. Matthews continues to count, reaches five and Richard remains fully conscious. His eyes are still slits, still black with hatred. Dr. Matthews thinks, then starts over: "Rick, I am going to count to ten. While I count, you are going to allow all the hatred you feel build up until you can't stand it. Then you are going to scream as loud as you can. Are you ready?"

"Yeah, sure."

"Okay, here goes." Dr. Matthews counts again. By the time he reaches four, Richard's entire body shakes. The wheelchair rattles against the floor. Dr. Matthews continues. At eight, Richard's mouth is fully open, his chin lifted toward the ceiling and he begins to groan. The groan grows louder and louder until at ten, it becomes a full-throated, deep-gutted scream. This scream from Richard reminds Dr. Matthews of the painting by the same name, the one with the deep, dark open mouth and the pale huge hands plastered to the sides of the sad face with the giant eyes. Rick's scream lasts less than a minute, but seems to go on for a considerable length of time. At its end, Rick cries without sobs; only with silent tears. He cries for perhaps ten minutes before he's completely exhausted. He appears deeply asleep in his wheelchair when he finally stops.

Dr. Matthews says, "I'm going to count backwards from five, Richard. When I get to one, you will wake up, feel totally refreshed. You will remember everything that happened this morning. You will understand your anger, but you won't hate your captors. Instead you will understand what they did to you and to your family. You will especially remember and understand what they did to your relationship with your brother, Charlie. And you will accept what they did to you and especially what they did to Charlie. You will accept these things because you can not change them, no matter how much you want to change them. Okay, are you ready to wake up?"

Rick violently shakes his head. "I'm afraid."

"Don't be," says the doctor. "Ready?"

Reluctantly Rick says, "I am."

Dr. Matthews counts backwards. When he reaches one, Richard wakes up. He looks at the doctor, and the first thing he says is: "Thank you."

"We've got work ahead, so don't thank me yet," says the doctor.

54 - GOOD-BYE ANNIE-BELLE

From Riverfront Stadium in downtown Cincinnati, Gary drives the rental car into the heart of Chicago to the least expensive hotel he is able to find through a travel agency in New York City. The Howard Johnson Inn is along Lasalle Street near the historical society and Wrigley Field, and is not very far from the shore of Lake Michigan. The Windy City is particularly blustery as Gary parks the car, and helps Ann out of the passenger side. They check in. Gary pokes Ann gently with an elbow when he signs the guest register: "Dr. & Dr. Gary Holden." Annie grins. *Doctor of Pharmacy, Doctor of Medicine.*

They settle themselves in a somewhat tacky bridal suite. Gary draws a hot bath for Ann as she's tired of traveling and wants to get into her pajamas, crawl in bed, watch some television. While Ann soaks in the tub, Gary opens his suitcase, pulls out a bottle of cheap red table wine and two plastic wine glasses he finds in a dime store in Brooklyn. He opens the wine with the corkscrew he almost forgets to pack, pours the dark red liquid into one of the glasses, knocks on the bathroom door and begins to turn the knob.

From behind the barrier, Ann speaks, "Gary!"

The door is locked. He stands there, surprised. "Unlock the door, baby. I've got something for you."

"Can't it wait?"

"Well, it can; but, I think you'll enjoy it now."

"Okay," she says. "Just a second."

Gary hears her get out of the water, then the door unlocks. He opens it. Ann stands on the bath mat, wrapped securely in a hotel towel.

He reaches out to her with the wine glass. With her free hand she takes it. "Oh, thanks sweetheart," she says. "Where's yours?"

"Out there."

"Well go get it," says Annie.

"Okay." Gary leaves, comes back with his glass of wine and the bottle which he places on the tile floor of the bathroom. Then he begins to strip. Annie grins. She removes the towel, steps back into the warm water, sits down into the tub. Gary, now naked, joins her. They toast each other's health and giggle like school kids. The wine, though inexpensive, tastes relatively good. Gary has a knack for picking decent wines with limited funds.

"This is nice," says Annie.

Gary puts his plastic glass on the floor, leans in close to Annie to kiss her neck. He moves up slowly to her mouth and gently licks her lips, keeping his tongue light on her skin. She responds, then takes a moment to free herself of her wine glass. Then, she is in her husband's lap. The young couple join together only for the second time of their brief marriage and their long relationship.

"I was so afraid," says Gary, "that we'd never get here."

"Here?"

"To this point."

Annie tears up. She kisses Gary's closed eyes, then his forehead, then moves to kiss each of his shoulders. She whispers, "I love you so much."

Annie-belle?

What is it, Charlie? Annie is aware she sounds annoyed.

Good-bye.

Annie stops kissing Gary. She listens.

Gary asks, "What?"

"Nothing," she says. *Charlie?*

Charlie repeats himself. *Good-bye, Annie.*

Annie says, *Wait.*

Charles Michael Logan walks along the edge of the railroad bridge that crosses the Cooper River from Charleston to Mount Pleasant. Below the bridge and above the river, pelicans fly low in a group. In the distance, the Atlantic Ocean shimmers. The early morning sun rises out of the horizon. A fog hangs over the last island before the shoreline.

Charlie sighs, well aware of Gary's presence. *I feel like an intruder. It's time to let go.* From this point forward, Charlie decides to speak only to his memory of Annie. But before he shuts his voice off from her mind, Charlie tells Annie of his plan: *It's important to move on, Annie-belle. It's time I let you go. I'm in the way of your life. And that's unfair.*

Annie listens again. *Charlie?*

Her older brother offers a little more. *You're right, Annie. I'm not going to lose it. I promise. No need for you to worry. I've found a way to live without you.*

Annie protests, *Don't leave me, Charlie. Please.* She gets no response.

At first Annabelle doesn't fully notice, but by the next afternoon the absence of Charlie's voice becomes loud and clear. This new, unexpected silence is deafening. Annie keeps trying to reach her brother but he doesn't respond. Throughout the remainder of the evening, Ann is gloomy. She knows this is unfair to Gary; but she can't throw off the oddly heavy loneliness she feels without Charlie's presence.

To Gary, Ann seems to go missing suddenly. Nevertheless, he decides he must wait patiently for his new wife to return. But, he's afraid. Ann is not the same person he knows. *She's not the woman I married.*

Late that night, her husband is especially sweet and Annie tries very hard to come back into their honeymoon. She allows Gary to make love to her, but in the morning Gary finds himself alone in the bed. Annie is in the shower when he wakes. He thinks nothing of it although he feels a little awkward by himself in the particularly large bridal suite bed. He rises, turns on the television, crawls back under the covers and waits for his wife to come out of the bathroom.

The local news is ordinary this morning; not much happening in the Chicago area. Gary thinks ahead. Today, he plans to take Ann to the Art Institute of Chicago to see George Seurat's famous painting, *A Sunday Afternoon on the Island of La Grande Jatte.* Gary sees and admires this work of art in books but never in person. He is excited to stand before this piece and see it for himself. He also anticipates sharing this unique experience with his wife, the woman he loves.

In the shower stall, Annie cries. She does so deliberately in a concerted effort to fully experience her now total loss of Charlie. Abruptly and before she gets out from underneath the hot stream of water, she begs Charlie to come back. But he doesn't speak to her. After listening for his voice for a few minutes, Annie gives up, turns off the water, steps out of the stall, dries off. She stands in front of the sink, stares at her face in the foggy mirror, fakes a broad smile before she opens the bathroom door to exit.

A moment later, Ann comes out of the bathroom in a robe, slightly open in front. Gary sees she's been crying. He also sees the smooth skin of her bare torso, which arouses him again. "Come here, darling." She comes to him, sits on the edge of the bed, kisses him. He puts his hand on her, and brings her close. They make love again. Annie's passion is more evident this morning than last night, and Gary is relieved. His trepidation subsides a little.

Afterwards Annie watches the news while Gary showers. A few times, she lowers the volume of the television to listen for Charlie, but again he doesn't speak to her. When Gary comes out of the bathroom, Annie forces a dry laugh, pats the mattress. Gary laughs, too. He says, "Well, it *is* our honeymoon."

The couple lounge around for an hour after making love again, until Annie says she's hungry. They dress, go to the lobby restaurant to eat a hearty breakfast. Then, they go to their rental car and Gary drives them to the Art Institute.

Gary leads Ann to the open hall in the center of the museum. As they enter, *A Sunday Afternoon* spans one end of the long room. Seurat's classic painting is huge, much larger than Gary imagines. The sight first from a distance, then up close and again at a distance brings him close to tears. Standing beside her husband, Annie feels his emotion in a way she never has before. She looks at him, then looks once more at the painting. She sees the life-size yet delicate women posing, holding parasols; the sturdy men lounging on the ground, smoking their long stem pipes. She notices the odd little monkey and the silky dogs, the patches of mellow green grass and bright green grass, and the many small boats with white sails on the still blue water. Annie thinks the scene in Seurat's grand impressionist painting is busy; yet peaceful and still. She glances at her husband who weeps silently. Annie clutches Gary's hand tightly in her own. She places her head on his shoulder, and smiles. Gary slides his arm around Ann's waist and gently squeezes. To both her absent brother and her present husband, Ann says, *Thank you.*

Annie then whispers, *Good-bye Charlie.*

ANNIE DREAMING

ABOUT THE AUTHOR

Carley Eason Evans earned her Master of Science degree in Speech Language and Auditory Pathology from East Carolina University, Greenville, North Carolina in 1993; and her Bachelor of Arts degree in English/Writing from Denison University, Granville, Ohio in 1976.

Carley lives in the greater Charleston area, and has two grown children. When not writing, she works as an acute care Speech Language Pathologist at the Medical University of South Carolina.

Carley has published poems and short stories in a variety of small literary magazines.

Carley Evans' first novel, METAL MAN WALKING was published on May 20, 2012. ANNIE DREAMING is her second novel in print.

ABOUT DOORFRAME BOOKS

METAL MAN WALKING is the first novel in the Doorframe book series and is a parallel story to **ANNIE DREAMING.**

Metal Man Walking follows 'Metal Man' Chuck a former baseball player who once dreams of becoming another Johnny Bench. Chuck struggles to overcome great odds in his desire to make some sort of life for himself on the streets of North Charleston. While searching these streets for anything of value, this homeless man finds an extraordinary item and makes a journey that although short is harrowing in the effort it requires of him. With new and unexpected resources at his disposal, Chuck checks in to a cheap, local motel where he relaxes in relative luxury. While there, he takes time to reflect on both the capricious and serendipitous events of his life, and to wonder where he might wind up tomorrow.

METAL MAN WALKING is widely available, including at CreateSpace and Amazon.com. Ask for it at your local bookstore and library.

Made in the USA
Lexington, KY
29 June 2014